THE SECRET D... OF PIXIE PIPER

Annabelle Fisher

ILLUSTRATIONS BY
Natalie Andrewson

Greenwillow Books
An Imprint of HarperCollinsPublishers

The Secret Destiny of Pixie Piper
Text copyright © 2016 by Annabelle Fisher
Illustrations copyright © 2016 by Natalie Andrewson

The text of this book is set in 11-point Arrus BT.
Book design by Paul Zakris

Library of Congress Cataloging-in-Publication Data
Names: Fisher, Annabelle, author. | Andrewson, Natalie, illustrator.
Title: The secret destiny of Pixie Piper / by Annabelle Fisher ;
    illustrations by Natalie Andrewson.
Description: First edition. | New York, NY : Greenwillow Books, [2016] |
    Summary: "Pixie Piper, an ordinary fifth grader, discovers she is a direct
    descendant of Mother Goose—and she has the magical ability and poetry
    power to prove it"— Provided by publisher.
Identifiers: LCCN 2016009230 | ISBN 9780062393784 (paperback)
Subjects: | CYAC: Elementary schools—Fiction. | Schools—Fiction. |
    Poetry—Fiction. | Secrets—Fiction. | Mother Goose—Fiction. | Characters
    in literature—Fiction.
Classification: LCC PZ7.1.F5676 Se 2016 | DDC [Fic]—dc23
LC record available at https://lccn.loc.gov/2016009230
17 18 19 20 21 OPM 10 9 8 7 6 5 4 3 2 1
First paperback edition, 2017

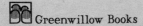 Greenwillow Books

For
Charlie,
Giles,
and Leo

CHAPTER ONE
Ye olde curse

When the Renaissance Faire came to town, Mom announced we had to go. She said it was my chance to "visit history" by observing what life in an English village was like in the days when there were lords and ladies, knights, archers, falconers, jugglers, peddlers, and peasants. But the truth was, Mom loved anything to do with costumes. I think she just couldn't resist seeing what the people at the fair would be wearing.

I reminded her that one of my favorite books was *Crispin: The Cross of Lead*, so I knew that back in those days most of the people were actually starving and dressed in rags. But Mom insisted that a Renaissance Faire was for fun and it wasn't going to focus on that part of history. Besides, she'd already decided she and my father were going as a milkmaid and a woodsman, and that Sammy, my baby brother, would be a mini jester.

I agreed to go, but I refused the long, velvet princess gown she wanted to make for me. Instead I was planning to wear jeans with my favorite green T-shirt. I was going as myself, Pixie Piper, fifth grader and citizen of modern times.

Although the fair was held on the grounds of an old farm where we'd once bought pumpkins and cornstalks, I didn't recognize the place. Now there were dirt-packed lanes filled with knights in armor, sorceresses peddling love potions, and jesters juggling eggs. It was like Mom had described, only better because I could hear the armor clanking and smell the spicy, mysterious potions. But when a wandering minstrel in purple pantaloons dropped to his knee to sing to me, I felt my neck turn red as rare roast beef. I didn't mind seeing history, but I didn't want to be a part of it.

My parents were different, though. While I stood on the sidelines and held Sammy's hand, Dad tried jousting and Mom joined a ladies' circle dance.

After Dad put on a plastic helmet and chest plate, a fake stableman helped him climb onto a grown-up size rocking horse named Sir Wobbles. Some other kid's father was sitting opposite Dad on an identical rocking horse named Sir Tipsy.

The stableman handed each of them a long silver lance. "The first one to knock his opponent off the saddle will be declared the winner," he announced.

At least the ground around the horses was covered with piles of hay.

"I'll lance your pants!" Dad shouted.

"I'll jab your flab!" the other father yelled back.

But the lances were as floppy as overcooked spaghetti. Both dads lost their balance and fell into the hay. The crowd jeered and hooted, but my dad clasped his hands overhead as if he'd been victorious. He actually took a bow.

Mom was okay at circle dancing, which was mostly clapping, curtsying, and skipping. She was just too enthusiastic. Every time the dancers changed direction, they were supposed to call, "Hey, ho!" Only Mom was so eager, she kept saying it too early. Even worse, she shrieked it like it was a battle cry: "HEYYY, HOOOOO!"

One day my parents were going to embarrass me to death.

Still, by the end of the afternoon, even I felt sorry to leave. That is, until Dad bought Sammy a giant, barbecued turkey leg at Ye Olde Drumstick Seller's. He took one bite and began waving it like a lance at me.

Before he managed to sauce me, I escaped over the wide, grassy field we'd crossed on our way in. I thought the rabbits and groundhogs that popped up everywhere like whack-a-moles might distract my brother. But by the time I reached the path to Ye Olde Parking Lot, he'd begun shrieking my name. It made me feel like a real stinker.

I was just about to turn back when I noticed a woman dressed in black, sitting in a rickety lawn chair to the side of the path. At her feet was a straw basket into which people had thrown coins and bills, and leaning against it was a shabby stuffed goose. She was talking on a sparkle-covered cell phone. The sight made me laugh out loud.

Quickly, she ended her call and dropped the cell phone in her lap.

"Hello there, poppet," she said.

"Are you supposed to be Mother Goose?" I asked as I took in the cone-shaped hat that sat atop her frizzy red hair and the old-timey cape that was tied under her chin.

"Verily I am her, see?" The woman pointed to her grungy goose. A sign hanging around its neck read:

RHYMES I TELL AND FORTUNES DIVINE.

TOSS IN A COIN, I'LL TELL THEE THINE.

Yeah right, I thought, eyeing the cell phone. Then I made up a rhyme of my own.

"Fortunes you tell, but not to me

I think you're full of ba-lo-ney!"

I didn't say it aloud, though. I'd given up writing poetry.

"Hello there," my father boomed as the rest of my family caught up. "Do you want to introduce us to your friend, Pixie?"

I gave him a look that meant, Seriously, Dad? But he just winked back. "This is Mother Goose," I said through gritted teeth.

"Duck!" Sammy chirped, grabbing the stuffed bird in his sticky hands.

"It's supposed to be a goose, Sammy—and you're getting it dirty." I snatched it back and dropped it in the woman's lap. My brother began to wail.

A large, hairy mole on her nose twitched as she glanced at me. But when she turned to Sammy, she was smiling. "Not to worry, sweetie. Goosey will get a bath when we get home." She held out a brown bag with the words PEANUT BUTTER WISH COOKIES on it. "Here," she said to me, "take a cookie for your brother and have one yourself."

Accepting cookies from a stranger didn't seem like a very good idea. "No thanks. We already ate a lot of snacks," I said. But my mother reached into the bag and took one. When she handed it to Sammy, he stopped crying.

The old woman turned to me with an oversize smile. "You can just take yours along for later." She wrapped one in a napkin and held it up.

"That's very thoughtful of you, Mother Goose," Mom said. She narrowed her eyes at me until I reached out and accepted the cookie.

"Thanks," I mumbled.

The woman nodded. Then she began rubbing her hands together as if I were next on the menu.

"A tisket, a tasket

A goose and a basket.

Your heart holds a question

And now you must ask it."

When she was done chanting, she raised an eyebrow and waited.

I opened my mouth but didn't say anything. I had a question, all right. But it was in my jeans pocket, not my heart. There was no way I was sharing it with her.

"I—I'm in fifth grade. I don't believe in fortunes."

"Bosh! No one is too old to have her fortune told." She closed her eyes and spoke in that singsong voice again:

"A rhyme in a pocket

A cinnamon curl

A secret uncovered

A Mother Goose Girl!"

Suddenly I felt something like a storm rising in my chest. Before I even knew what I was going to say, I shouted:

"Your fortune's just a big fat lie

'Cause I'm as normal as apple pie!"

Then I threw the cookie onto the ground so hard it must have broken into a thousand pieces, and ran.

CHAPTER TWO
Ye olde creepy coincidence

Ooh, my tongue was such a traitor! I couldn't believe
I'd answered that fortune-telling Mother Goose with
a rhyme. But I'd been really freaked out. The reason
was in my pocket—a verse I'd made up the night
before, even though I'd given up on poetry. Rhyming
was what I'd always done when I had trouble sleeping.

Fair day, fair day, who shall I see?

Archer, blacksmith, swordsman, three

Girls selling pork pies or marigold tea

Lady, maid, or *goose girl*, which shall I be?

How could that weird woman have known what I'd written?

"Pixie!" Suddenly Mom caught my elbow. "What's going on? Why were you so rude to that nice lady?"

"Didn't you hear her, Mom? She called me a 'Mother Goose Girl.' It was so mean!"

"Oh, honey, you're just being oversensitive." My mother's voice softened as she turned me to face her. "It was only a figure of speech. She didn't mean it literally. Lots of girls your age write poems."

Maybe she was right. Last week my best friend, Gray Westerly, had called me touchy. He'd always teased me, but lately it seemed to bother me more.

Dad caught up to us, carrying Sammy on his shoulders. "Hey, you two! Is something wrong?" he huffed.

Mom sent him a bright, easy smile. "No worries! Pixie was wondering why that fortune-teller called her a goose girl."

"I guess Mother Goose knows all, Pix," he said.

"Daddy! It's not funny!" I grumbled, although I wasn't really mad anymore. "Besides, her rhymes don't make any sense."

"Actually, many Mother Goose rhymes are based on history. They were a kind of secret code for protesting unfair rulers and their laws," said Mom.

Dad smiled. "Your mom's got more Mother Goose books than the library. She's practically an expert on the subject."

"Not really," Mom said, but she had a pleased look on her face.

"Well, I don't care!" I snapped. "I don't want to be like that woman. The mole on her nose was bigger than a blueberry!"

"Are you kidding? It was more like a small island! The hairs on it were as tall as palm trees!" Dad exclaimed.

"Shh!" Mom poked him. "For your information, that mole wasn't real, Pixie. It was probably made of Play-Doh."

"But it was growing hair!"

"Silly! That was cat hair—she had it all over her cape," said Mom. "She was playing a role, just like the other characters at the fair."

"She might be a good actress, but she needs a better prop. Her stuffed goose was lame." Dad winked at me.

"Phil!" Mom scolded. Then she burst into giggles. "She called it G-g-goosey," she sputtered.

On the car ride home, they made up silly

names for the goose, such as Din-din, Drumstick, Stewie, Eggbert, Bubba, Bigfoot, Butt Duster, Wing Nut, Gizzard, Gravy, Giblets, Jerky, Bacon, and Pillowsteak. My father was laughing so hard, I was afraid he'd drive off the road.

"What would you name it, Sammy?" he sputtered.

"Duck!" my baby brother crowed.

"How about you, Pix?" Dad asked as he pulled up beside our house. Sometimes he just couldn't give up a joke.

"I'd name it Nothing—'cause I'm never getting one!" Thank goodness we were finally home. Quickly, I flung open the car door and jumped onto the driveway before he asked me any more corny questions.

All I wanted was to be normal—the kind of girl who got invited to see Sage Green's golden retriever puppy and ate lunch at the table with the McMansion girls. Though with a family like mine, it hardly seemed possible.

CHAPTER THREE
Ye olde Backyard Bummer

Our house, Acorn Cottage, was halfway down a long, windy drive. It suited us the way an oddly shaped package sometimes holds a weird gift. The house got its name because the center of the roof looked like an acorn cap: round, with shingles set in a cross-hatch pattern, and a crooked chimney for the stem. The front door even had a small, acorn-shaped window made of amber-colored glass. I'd always loved our home, especially its round living room, which had three curved window seats that were great for reading or thinking. But lately, I'd been admiring the kind of big, modern houses a lot of the kids on my bus lived in. Most of them looked as if they could fit three Acorn Cottages inside.

"Some people call them McMansions," Mom said with a sniff when I mentioned it. "They're built to impress people, but who needs all those rooms?"

I hadn't meant to seem envious, but those houses were beautiful. I'd overheard some girls on the bus discussing the one that Sage Green, who was in my class, lived in. I'd been there once, but I'd only gotten as far as the coat closet.

"One room is a theater for watching movies," Sage's friend Maya announced. "The screen takes up a whole wall."

"Yeah, and it has seven bathrooms," Ellie added. "All of them have TVs, and showers that look like waterfalls!"

I would've liked *any* shower instead of the old claw-foot tub I had to climb into each night. But we lived in Acorn Cottage because it was on the Winged Bowl Estate where my dad was the caretaker. The big manor house owned by Mr. Timothy Bottoms was about a quarter mile farther down the winding drive. The property had gardens, fountains, woods, and a pond, which made it better than any back-yard or even playground. But it also had a museum. Which was the problem.

Why? Because it was a museum of toilets. You could call them potties, lavatories, johns, or commodes, but it didn't change what they were for. Mom called them "thrones" when she was being funny. But it wasn't funny—it was embarrassing.

Uncle Bottoms (who wasn't my real uncle, but acted like one) had built the museum when I was about four. When I was little, a toilet museum didn't seem any different than the dinosaur or art museums my parents had taken me to see. The truth was, I'd loved the toilet that was shaped like a teapot and the turtle one that had a potty underneath its shell.

But when I began riding the school bus, that all changed. Some of the bigger kids said I lived at "Winged Butt" instead of Winged Bowl. Or they called Acorn Cottage "The Outhouse." I knew that Mac, our driver, would have made them walk if he'd heard, but I didn't want to cause trouble. And any-way, we all went to Winged Bowl Elementary and Middle School, so the jokes stopped as soon as the bus arrived. You could say we were all in the bowl together.

But when I got to third grade, a fifth grader on my bus named Hugo Tucker called me Princess Potty. His brother, Raffi, who was in my class, hee-hawed like a donkey at the stupid joke.

"*Princess Potty! Princess Potty!*" some other kids on the bus started shouting as they twisted around to look at me.

Tears stung my eyes. I willed them not to fall.

In the seat beside me, my friend Gray hissed, "Ignore those jerks, Pix. It could be a lot worse. Like, you could be living next to the thirty-foot-tall statue of a pistachio nut they've got in Alamogordo, New Mexico. Then the kids would be calling you Nutty."

"Ha-ha," I grumbled. "Not worse."

"No, really!" Gray insisted. "Did you know that in Enterprise, Alabama, there's a gigantic replica of a boll weevil on top of a monument? If that one were in your backyard, they'd be calling you Buggy."

This time I giggled for real. "I guess you're right," I said, though I still thought Princess Potty was worse. But I ignored the jerks—that is, until the bus got to my stop. On my way off, I kicked them.

"Why does Uncle Bottoms even need a stupid toilet museum?" I'd asked Dad when I got home.

He looked up from tinkering with something on his workbench. "The museum is like his trophy room and the toilets are his trophies," he said. "Mr. B. earned his fortune by creating a website called The Winged Bowl that shows where the best public bathrooms all over the world are located."

"Who cares about that?" I'd grumbled.

Dad scratched the back of his neck with a screwdriver. "Apparently millions of travelers do, Pix. So to show his gratitude, Mr. B. founded the Museum of Rare, Historical, and Unique Toilets. He felt we should all know how much we owe our health to the development of toilet technology."

"Big whoop," I muttered, but he just smiled.

"Why don't you try skipping stones on the pond until you feel better?"

I did try it. And he was right—sort of. Skipping stones can change the way you look at things. I didn't love the museum, but I loved the people in charge of it—my dad and Uncle Bottoms. After the Princess Potty episode, the museum and I mostly ignored each other.

CHAPTER FOUR
Ye olde secret

The night after we got home from the Renaissance Faire, Mom came into my room. "Can we talk, Pixie?"

"Sure." I scrunched over in bed so she could sit beside me.

She smoothed out a wrinkle in my quilt. "I know lately you've been feeling different—"

"It's okay," I interrupted. "I know what happened today was just a coincidence. That fortune-telling Mother Goose was just a faker."

Mom hesitated a moment. "Well, probably."

Probably? That was weird. A cold finger of fear traced my spine.

"There's something I need to tell you. I've been waiting until you were old enough to hear the truth—but I think I may have waited too long."

I burrowed down deeper under my quilt. My mother had been keeping a secret from me. A truth so terrible, she'd waited years to tell me. I wanted to put my hands over my ears, but I was too old for that kind of stuff. "Okay, what?" I croaked.

"Well . . . ," she said. She took a deep breath and looked up at the stars on my ceiling. "You are a descendant."

"Isn't that like an ancestor?"

"No, ancestors are the people who came before you—a line stretching way back in time. Descendants are their children, grandchildren, great-grandchildren and so on."

"But everyone is a descendant!"

"Yes, but you"—Mom tapped my nose as if I were still a little kid—"are a descendant of someone extraordinary."

"Extraordinary"? Did she mean special—or strange? I swallowed hard. "Who?"

She patted my leg. "This is going to sound a little crazy, but it's important that you know, because, well . . ."

"Just tell me, Mom!"

"Okay." She took another deep breath and let it out. "You're a descendant of Mother Goose. I am too, but I don't have her powers. At least, not anymore."

"Ha-ha, very funny. Mother Goose is a fairy-tale character. She doesn't have powers—she makes up nursery rhymes."

Mom folded the edge of the quilt away from my face. She'd made it out of leftover fabric from her many costumes and it was crazy and beautiful. "Oh, Pixie. Apparently there's a lot more to it. My mama used to tell me that I was special and that someday a group of descendants called the Goose Ladies would come for me. She said they would teach me how to use my power."

Okay, my mother was unusual even when she wasn't talking about imaginary people. But this was just plain weird. "Come on, Mom, I'm too old for this stuff."

"Pixie, I'm serious." There wasn't even a hint of a smile on her face.

"But who are they? What do they do?" The idea

that a bunch of weird women with hairy warts might be coming for me was scary. I looked around my room, wondering if they would suddenly fly in through the window or walk through the wall—and if there was any way to stop them.

"Only the Goose Ladies know about the Goose Ladies," she said with a sorry little shrug. "I don't think my mama wanted to tell me much until I was older."

"She never said *anything* else about them?"

"Well, there was this one rhyme she taught me. We'd say it together before I went to sleep."

"Do you still remember it?"

She nodded and closed her eyes.

> "Fragile, light, and sturdy
> To house a little birdie
> Or enclose a tiny sun
> Then it cracks—and hope's begun!"

When Mom opened her eyes again, they had a faraway look in them. "I never got a chance to learn what it meant because of the car crash."

My throat welled up whenever Mom spoke of her childhood. She'd only been five when her parents died. I reached out and took her hand.

"After I was living with my grandparents for a

while, I began to suspect that my grandma knew something," she said. "One day she swooped into my room and gathered up all my nursery rhyme books. I never saw them again."

"Is that why you collect them now?" Mom had an entire shelf of Mother Goose books in her room.

She sent me a crooked smile. "Actually, I did manage to hide one of the old ones from my grandma."

"Really? Do you still have it?"

"I do. Unfortunately, it isn't a very good one," she replied.

"Can I see it?"

"Another time. It's getting late." She started to rise, but I grabbed her hand. There was still something I needed to know.

"Did you ever see them, Mom?"

"No," she said, sighing deeply. "I used to think it was because I was never alone—my grandma never let me go anywhere without her. Although as I grew older, I wondered if the Goose Ladies were just part of a tale my mama made up."

"But what do you believe now?"

She played with my fingers for a moment. "I think someday they'll come for you—because of your rhymes, you know? Mine were never as good as yours. For years while I was at Grandma's, I used to wish they'd appear. That's why I'm so excited for you now."

I didn't tell her I'd given up on poetry because it made me seem like a weirdo. I was afraid it would hurt her feelings.

"What does Dad think about the, um, Goose Ladies?" I asked.

"Oh, Pixie, he doesn't know! Mama always said it was important to keep them a secret from outsiders."

On top of the bookcase Dad had built for me, there was a framed photo of my parents, taken before I was born. In it, the two of them were licking a single mint chip ice cream cone. I couldn't believe she hadn't told him. They'd always shared everything. How could she call him an outsider?

I twisted some strands of hair around my finger. "So that fortune-teller at the fair today—do you think she's one of them?"

"Oh, no." Mom shook her head. "She was too conspicuous. Too loud. I doubt that they wear costumes. Probably they want to keep themselves hidden." She cupped my chin with a gentle hand. "It's really important that you never mention this to anyone. I need you to promise."

"I won't tell anyone," I whispered. "I promise."

Because really, who would have believed it anyway?

The next day, while Mom was outside gardening, I went into her room and found what looked like the book she'd hidden from her grandma. It was the only one that didn't have a paper cover with a picture of a lady in a tall black hat or a fat white goose wearing old-fashioned spectacles on it. This cover was soft brown leather. Although some letters in the title were worn away, I could still make out what it said: *Sister Goose's Cautionary Verse for Brats.*

"Sister Goose"? "Brats"? I took the book into my room and closed the door. On the first page was a rhyme I'd never read or heard before:

> *Each and every moral rhyme*
> *The little child should keep in mind.*
> *But if a brat does not obey*
> *Punishment shall rule the day.*

The last line gave me goose bumps. Was it some kind of warning? I shut the book and shoved it under my pillow. If any Goose Ladies tried to come for me, I'd throw it at them.

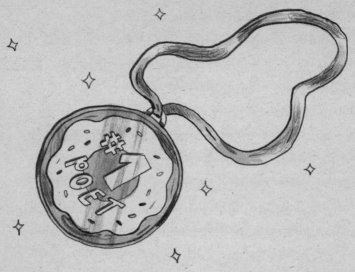

CHAPTER FIVE
Ye olde Golden Donut

Although our school was named after flying toilets, it was a pretty awesome place. Uncle B. had donated enough money for the students of Winged Bowl to have a super-modern facility with the very latest technology. We all got our own laptops. The cafeteria food was actually edible, and we even grew some of it ourselves on our rooftop farm. The schoolyard had a ropes course, a zip line, and a climbing wall. We even had the most modern toilets—the seats were heated in cold weather, they were compostable to save water, and best of all, they were smell-free.

The first thing Monday morning, our principal, Ms. Mosely, had us gather in the auditorium for what she called "a wonderful surprise." She used the words "wonderful" and "special" a lot.

"Since Winged Bowl School is such a special place, I've decided it should have a poet laureate," she announced. "A poet laureate is appointed by a president, a king, or a queen to get the citizens excited about reading and discussing poetry. And most wonderful of all, a poet laureate writes poems to honor his or her country's special occasions."

I could practically hear what the kids around me were thinking—Big whoop.

"At Winged Bowl, we are going to have a poetry contest to select our special poet," Ms. Mosely continued. "He or she will write poems in honor of important school observances, such as Dental Health Month, Egg Salad Week, Head Lice Awareness Day, Thumb Appreciation Day, Teacher Appreciation Day, Substitute Teacher Appreciation Day, and Principal Appreciation Day."

There were so many snorts and snickers, the auditorium sounded like a stable full of horses. The teachers had to stand up and shoot dirty looks at the troublemakers.

But Ms. Mosely was still smiling. "Now I know you're all going to want to enter the contest," she said. "Especially since our benefactor, Mr. Bottoms, has commissioned a medal for our poet laureate to wear." She opened a black box that was resting on the podium and lifted out a gold medal on a striped ribbon that was like the kind Olympic athletes got for winning. A few of the kids stood to get a better look at the medal, which resembled a golden donut.

Big whoop.

I watched Ms. Mosely watching us with raised eyebrows. I knew she wanted us to applaud, but the kids around me were acting like their fingers had turned into worms. Dead worms. Since I'd given up writing poetry, I didn't care much, either. But as I watched her eyebrows sink, I couldn't help feeling sorry for her.

"Come on, let's make some noise," I whispered to Gray, who was sitting next to me.

"Okay, sure," he agreed. Then he burped as if he were running for burper laureate.

"Not like that!" I started clapping really hard to cover up for him.

But at the sound of Gray's gigantic eruption, the kids around us burst into applause. Ms. Mosely's smile returned. She must have thought they were clapping for the golden donut.

"Maybe I'll enter," Gray whispered. "I could use that thing as a hockey puck."

But my attention had wandered away. Even though I'd vowed not to write any more poems, my disobedient brain was already making one up:

> *Dental health's boring*
> *But if it's forgotten*
> *Your breath will smell doggy*
> *And your teeth will get rotten.*

In my imagination, I saw myself accepting the medal. Then I realized I was wearing a black cape and carrying a basket with an ugly stuffed goose in it. It wasn't a daydream—it was a daymare!

"Hey, are you choking? You're turning purple," said Gray. He began pounding my back.

"S-s-stop!" I sputtered, swatting him away. "I just need some water." Holding my throat, I squeezed out of the aisle with everyone watching. That's when I began thinking, *What if that wacky Mother Goose's curse was real?*

I was already settled at the back of the school bus when Gray dropped down next to me. We lived

across the road from each other and we'd been riding the bus together since kindergarten. I probably
spent more time with him than with my parents.

"So are you entering the contest?" he asked as the
bus lurched away from school.

"What contest?"

"The poet laureate contest. Did you leave your
brain in your locker?"

I looked around to see if anyone had heard him,
but most of the kids were busy talking, trading
snacks, or glued to their music or games.

Sage Green and her friends Maya, Anna, and Ellie
were cooing over something—probably photos of
Sage's golden retriever puppy.

"No way."

"Why not?"

"Because I don't want to, Gray. I hate writing
poetry."

"What? Since when?"

"Since now!" I snapped, more sharply than I'd
meant to.

Gray's answer to that was a burp. Then he put his
earbuds in and ignored me.

Right away, I felt sorry. The truth was, ever since
we were little I'd entertained both of us with rhymes

about all the stuff we did together. We liked to compete over everything—who could get a better grade, catch the most popcorn on their tongue, or run the fastest.

I could still remember a poem I made to tease him when we were seven or eight:

Pix and Gray ran up a hill
To see who would be faster.
Pix bumped a tree and skinned her knee
So Gray became the master.

Then down they raced on speedy legs
Once again competing.
But this time Pix was extra quick
And ran past Gray to beat him.

Although I knew I deserved it, I hated having Gray mad at me. As soon as we got off the bus, I'd explain to him why I wasn't entering the contest. I reached into my backpack for my book and found a cookie in a plastic baggie instead. My stomach dropped as if the bus had gone over a giant bump. Right away I knew it was one of the "peanut butter wishes." Had the fake Mother Goose fortune-teller—or whatever she was—somehow slipped it into my bag?

Okay, I knew that was crazy. Mom must have

packed it as an extra snack. It was just a cookie. So I held it under Gray's nose.

"Hey, want this?"

He was still acting as if I weren't there.

Strangely, the cookie's sweet, nutty scent began to make my mouth water. I couldn't resist taking a tiny bite. It melted on my tongue like a puff of cotton candy.

"I wish something exciting would happen today," I murmured, even though I didn't believe a peanut-butter cookie could grant a wish any more than a fortune cookie could tell a fortune. I plucked one of Gray's earbuds from his ear. "Hey, do you want to go down to the pond later?"

I thought he was still ignoring me. But then he slid his eyes sideways and cracked a slight grin. "Yeah, okay."

"Cool." I stuck the earbud back into his ear. That's when I noticed Sage watching us.

CHAPTER SIX
Ye olde Phone call

When the bus pulled up at our stop, I leaped off the steps. Gray was right behind me. "I'll drop my stuff at home and tell my grandma where I'm going," he yelled. "Be over in a few minutes." His house was right across the road from our driveway.

"Okay, hurry!" I didn't want to miss a minute of the sunny spring day. I was hoping to see some rabbit kits or a roly-poly groundhog cub. And those tiny, wild strawberries that grew in the woods might be ripe, although Gray broke out in hives if he ate too many.

"Peeksie, Peeksie!" Sammy chirped from his high chair when I entered the kitchen. He waved a grape-juice Popsicle at me.

I loved how he said my name. I loved everything about him. I'd been nine years old when he was born. Sometimes it felt as if Mom, Dad, and I had been holding our breath until he came along.

"Hi, Sammy." I took a pretend lick of his drippy Popsicle and patted his head, which was sticky as usual. "Hi, Mom. Whose is that?" She was at the kitchen table, sewing buttons on a very large, very pink sweater. Most days she got home a little earlier than me and picked up Sammy from Gray's grandma, who was his babysitter. Afterward she usually mended clothes or ran errands for the residents at the nursing home where she worked.

"It belongs to Kitty Beans. Her arthritis makes it hard for her to sew." She put down the sweater and gave me a hug. "How was your day?"

"Fine. Is it okay if I go down to the pond with Gray and do my homework after?"

"Sure." She looked up for a sec. "Oh, you had a phone call."

"Who was it?"

"Sage Green. I told her you weren't home yet and

that you'd call her back." Mom tore a sheet off the pad where she'd written Sage's number.

Was Sage going to invite me over to see her new puppy? That's where the other girls on the bus had been going. Maybe she was sorry she hadn't asked me, too. It was silly, but I couldn't help thinking that it might be the exciting thing I'd wished for.

"Do you want a Popsicle?" asked Mom.

"No thanks. I guess I'll call Sage now." I took the phone into the living room so I could curl up in a window seat while I talked. For privacy, I pulled the purple velvet drapes closed around me. I didn't call right away, though. I wanted to see the puppy, but after what happened at Sage's tenth birthday party, I didn't ever want to be around her mother again.

Sage had invited everyone in the class. Although I'd felt a little nervous, I'd been excited about getting to see her house. I'd only gotten as far as the gigantic coat closet in the hall when I'd overheard Mrs. Green talking to someone in the kitchen. "Dana Piper is awfully colorful. You should see the costumes she wears to the nursing home where my mother lives."

Since she was talking about my mom, I froze and listened.

"I know! Last week I saw her at the grocery store

wearing a ball gown and a tiara," the other person agreed. "I pretended not to notice her."

My mom, Dana, was a recreation therapist at the Good Old Days, which was a residence for seniors. Her job was to plan activities that were both entertaining and therapeutic. She often wore gowns, capes, hats, tiaras, and other unusual clothes to work. "My costumes remind the residents of the parties they attended and the places they visited. It gives them something to talk about, and it stimulates their memories," she'd once explained to me.

Sometimes, when she was in a hurry, Mom stopped at the grocery store on her way home from work. She couldn't help it if she was still wearing a wedding gown or a tutu. I thought I might explain that to Sage's mother later, when the other woman was gone. But then Mrs. Green said, "Well, look at how she dresses her daughter—all those homemade clothes. I don't think that child owns a pair of jeans."

Before anyone knew I'd arrived, I grabbed my jacket and slipped back outside. I was wearing a soft, blue velvet skirt Mom had sewn and a shirt she'd decorated with blue jay feathers. In the wrapped box I was carrying, there was another shirt just like it that Mom had made for Sage. I went down the road and ditched the gift behind someone else's hedge. Then I waited behind a bush until Mom came back for me.

Though I never told her why, I stopped wearing all of the pretty skirts and tops Mom had made for me. I had two pairs of jeans and I wore one of them every day. But it didn't change anything. None of the girls in my class ever invited me over anyway— until maybe now.

I breathed deeply until I felt calm enough to call.

"Hi," I said as casually as if Sage and I phoned each other all the time. "How's your puppy?"

"She's chewing Ellie's sneaker lace right now."

I laughed as I pictured it. "She sounds like fun. I wish I had a puppy."

"Yah, Angel is super-cute," Sage agreed. "She's even got a pedigree."

"What's that?"

"Papers that show she's a pure golden retriever and tell who her parents were. Her mother was a grand champion."

Big whoop, I thought. But I only said, "I like her name."

"Thanks." Sage seemed to hesitate a moment. "Could I ask you something, Pixie?"

I pretended to think about it. "Um, sure." If Mom agreed to drive me, I could be at her door in five minutes!

Sage giggled. "It's kind of personal."

"That's okay," I said, but a funny flicking started up in my throat.

"Is Graham your boyfriend?" Sage was the only person in school who called Gray by his full name. He was in kindergarten when he'd decided he was only going to answer to the name Gray, because some of the kids had been calling him Graham Cracker.

"No. Of course he's not!"

"Well, you two are always together at lunch and on the bus, so I thought . . . *you know*. Don't you think he's cute?" In the background I could hear Sage's friends laughing.

"Gray's just my neighbor."

"Really? Are you sure?"

"Of course I'm sure!" The call was beginning to feel like a mean prank.

"Sorry, I was just wondering. But I believe you."

Gee, thanks, I thought. But I didn't say anything and neither did she. It was pretty uncomfortable. Finally, I couldn't stand it anymore. "I have to go now," I told her.

"Yah, me, too. It's time to walk the puppy."

I was about to hang up when I heard her say, "Maybe you can come over and see Angel sometime."

"Sure. When?"

"Um, I'll call you."

I had the feeling I'd just taken some sort of friendship test and flunked. After I hung up, I looked at myself in the mirror over the fireplace. Maybe cinnamon was nice sprinkled on applesauce, but as a hair color it was boring. Not red or brown, but a color that always looked faded. Sage had hair like black silk. Popular-girl hair. And unlike my unruly cinnamon curls, hers hung perfectly straight down her back.

"Hey, let's go!"

It was Gray. Mom must have let him in. Quickly I kneeled down and retied a sneaker lace so he wouldn't see me blushing. "Coming in a sec," I mumbled.

The truth was, I'd forgotten about him when I thought Sage was going to ask me over, even though he was my best friend. And my only friend.

CHAPTER SEVEN
Ye olde egg

Without discussing it, Gray and I took the path through the woods to the pond. We could have walked it with our eyes closed, but we didn't want to miss anything. Usually the air was noisy with tweets, quacks, and the flapping of wings, though sometimes you could catch the splashing of turtles and fish. But today it was hard to hear anything over the noise of the spring peepers, which were little bitty frogs the size of gummy bears.

"First one to spot one gets this," I said, pulling

a bloodred cardinal feather out of my sweatshirt pocket. Those peepers were the most frustrating things! The males called to the females constantly with high, shrill whistles, until you tried to find them. Then they got as silent as bumps on a log— which in a way, they were.

Gray crouched down to examine the nearest tree stump. I just watched. Sage had asked if I thought he was cute, but I'd known him so long, I wasn't sure. He had curly black hair and blue-gray eyes. He also had the worst-smelling sneakers in existence (which he called his "ultimate secret weapons"). And he liked burping way too much.

"Found one!" he exclaimed, pointing to what looked like a raisin with two eyes and four legs.

"Okay, here," I sighed, handing him my feather.

He twirled it around in his fingers for a moment. "Can I ask you something?"

It was beginning to feel like Ask Pixie Day, but I nodded anyway.

"Why did you get so mad on the bus when I asked you about running for poet laureate?"

"Because I don't want to be the girl who lives at Winged Butt *and* writes weird poems. I just want to be like everyone else. Normal."

"Then you should quit being so sensitive." He cracked a lopsided grin. "Anyway, you're not normal."

"Ha-ha." I breathed in deeply, taking in the sharp scent of new leaves and damp earth. I wanted so badly to tell him he was right. If he knew about the Goose Ladies and the fortune I'd been told, maybe he'd understand.

"You know that Renaissance Faire I went to last weekend?" I began. "Well, there was this weird woman dressed like Mother Goose who was telling fortunes. When I refused to let her tell mine, I think she put a curse on me."

Gray plucked a leaf off a shrub. "A grumpy spell?"

"I'm serious! She called me a Mother Goose Girl."

"Ha! Maybe she really is psychic. I bet you told her off with a rhyme."

"Yeah, sort of." My interest in sharing anything real about the Goose Ladies was already fading. I didn't like being laughed at. Besides, breaking my promise to Mom was making me feel guilty.

"Shh, Pix, listen!" Gray jerked his chin toward the tall grasses at the edge of the pond. "I think there's something hiding down by the water."

My stomach leaped like I'd swallowed a frog. Then I heard it, too—a rustling sound.

"Wait!" I grabbed the back of his T-shirt.

"What?"

Cheeks burning, I shrugged and dropped it. I was furious at myself for letting the Goose Ladies thing get to me. "Nothing. Go," I muttered. "I'll follow you."

Suddenly I saw a flash of red fur and a white-tipped tail in the grass. It was a fox! I stopped, but Gray kept creeping closer until the mud under his sneakers made a sucking sound. Instantly the fox popped up and saw us. I guess it was as startled as I'd been, because it jumped into the pond and began swimming away. When it reached the other side, it disappeared into the brush.

Neither of us said a word until it was gone. Then Gray let out a whoop. "I've never seen a fox swim before. That was awesome!"

"I know. Me, either." I searched the grass where the fox had been to see if there might be a clump of soft, red fur left behind. Instead, there was an egg.

"Gray, look!"

"I bet Mr. Fox was planning on having an omelet," he said.

"Or Mrs. Fox was bringing it to her kits."

I leaned down and touched the shell. "It's still

warm. The fox probably stole it from a duck's nest right around here someplace. Let's see if we can find it and put it back." I lifted the egg carefully and weighed it in my hand. It was bigger than my palm and felt surprisingly heavy.

We walked all the way around the pond without finding a nest hidden among the shrubs or tall grass.

"We'd better bring it to your dad. He'll know what to do." Lately Gray had been acting as if my dad were a fixer-upper celebrity like the guy on *Extremely Extremely Extreme Home Makeovers*.

"What's he going to do, sit on it?" I loved my father, but sometimes I wished he did something that required him to wear clothes like Mr. Westerly instead of the embarrassing farmer overalls he wore every day. Gray's father, Rob, was an editor of novels and poetry books. He was nice and fun, but last year he and Gray's mom, Amanda, whom I liked, too, had gotten a divorce. After his mom moved away, Gray's grandma had moved in with him and his dad.

"C'mon, hurry!" Gray said, heading toward the barn where my dad had his workshop.

I waited until he got a little farther away before I

lifted the egg up to my lips and whispered the rhyme
that had just nested in my brain.

"Little egglet on your own,

Have your mom and daddy flown?

Don't worry—you are not alone!

We'll find you a good safe home."

CHAPTER EIGHT
Ye Olde Egg Salad

It was dark as a moonless night in the coat closet where I was crammed with Gray, Sammy, and Dad. The itchy wool sleeve of Mom's winter coat kept brushing my face as if a ghost were playing a joke. But the boys were too busy watching Dad's science trick to care if I was freaking out. He'd taped an empty toilet paper roll to a flashlight and was shining the light beam it created onto the egg.

"Take a look at those veins pulsing inside the yolk sac," said Dad, pointing to some spidery lines. "That means the egg's been fertilized."

"Mine!" my brother exclaimed, trying to grab it.

"Not this one, Sammy." Dad raised the egg out of his reach. "Did you actually see the fox drop this, Pix? Because it's amazing that it didn't crack."

"No, but I found it where the fox was standing before it jumped into the water," I told him. "Where else could it have come from?"

"How 'bout the grocery store?" Gray joked.

"Ha-ha," I said without taking my eyes off the egg. It was amazing that you could actually see inside the shell. "What's that dark spot, Dad?"

"It's an embryo that hopefully will become a goose."

I grabbed Mom's coat for support as my knees began to shake. "A goose? I thought it was a duck egg!"

"It's too big to be a duck egg, Pix," Dad replied. "It was probably laid by one of the Canada geese that visit the pond."

"But couldn't there be a big, fat duckling inside?" I asked. "I once saw a woman on TV who gave birth to a fourteen-pound baby. His arms and legs looked like they were made out of salamis."

"I don't think that happens in the duck world,

Pixie. Anyway, since you didn't find its nest, we'll probably never know."

"What do you mean?"

"Well, if you don't want to raise a gosling, you should just put the egg back near the pond and let nature take its course."

It was a good thing it was dark in the closet. I felt myself getting red-faced and tears squeezed out of the corners of my eyes. "But we can't just let it die, Dad!"

"Oowah-oowah," Sammy began whimpering. Whenever I sounded upset, he cried.

"It's okay," I said, putting my arm around him. "Daddy's going to save Egg, right, Dad?"

My father sighed really loudly. "We could try to hatch it if that's what you want. It wouldn't be hard to construct a simple incubator."

"I could help you build it," Gray volunteered.

"That would be great. But even in an incubator, it would need daily attention. Are you willing to take care of the egg, Pixie?"

For a moment I didn't answer. Unlike a cute golden retriever puppy that other girls could coo over, I was going to get a pet egg. And then a goose. That hairy-moled fortune-teller's prophecy was coming true.

Gray poked me in the ribs. "Come on, say yes. Since we found it together, I'm sort of its dad."

"Oh, all right," I agreed. "Just don't call me its mother."

"Here, you can start now." Dad placed the egg in my hands. Then he opened the closet door. "Keep it warm while Gray and I set up the incubator."

"But how?"

"Use that big imagination of yours." Dad marched toward the front door with Gray and Sammy right behind him. "No Samster, you stay here and help Pixie," he said before my brother could squeeze outside.

"Egg would be a lot safer if Sammy went with you," I told him.

But Dad only grinned. "Mom ran out for milk. She should be home soon. Take care of both of your charges until then."

A few minutes later Sammy, Egg, and I were sitting in Mom's rocking chair. I held Sammy on my lap, he held a pillow on his, and Egg was nestled on top like a cherry in whipped cream.

"Pet Egg a little more softly please, Sammy," I whispered as we rocked in the chair.

"Please try not to jiggle Egg, Sammy."

"Don't hug Egg, Sammy!"

"SAMMY! DON'T KISS EGG AGAIN!"

I pried the egg from his hands as gently as I could. It was still nice and warm, which made me relax a little. I imagined I could even feel the shell vibrating under my touch.

"Sammy, do you want me to tell you a poem about another egg that got jiggled too much?" I asked.

He snuggled back against me, which meant yes. I was planning to recite Humpty Dumpty, but this is what came out instead:

"When Humpty D fell off the wall
The king's men gathered round.
'How shall we prepare him
Now that he's cracked his crown?'

"Fry him up in butter
Or scramble him with cheese,
But do not boil and chop him
Into egg salad, please!

"For if Prince Sammy finds it
In his sandwich, he will wail.
He'll toss the mess against the wall
And send you off to jail!"

Sammy clapped his hands. "Maww!" he demanded. So I repeated my poem over and over until he dozed off in my lap. Then I reached out and gave Egg a tiny flick with my fingernail.

"Did I find you or did you find me, Egg?" I whispered. But, *ha-ha*, it wasn't talking.

CHAPTER NINE
ye olde Dumb idea

The next morning, Gray was already waiting for the bus when I arrived at the end of the driveway. "How's Egg?" he asked.

"Okay. I turned it over and misted it like my dad said. It has to be kept moist the way it would be in a real nest. Usually the mom's damp feathers do the job."

We were using an old fish tank for the incubator and shredded newspaper for the nest. Dad had rigged up a high-intensity lamp and a thermometer, so we could keep the temperature inside the tank cozy, but not too hot. And to keep it out of Sammy's reach, it was on a worktop in the mudroom, which doubled as our laundry room.

"Did your dad say when it would hatch?"

"We read that it takes twenty-eight to thirty days. But we don't exactly know how long Egg's been an egg. I'll call you when I see—" I interrupted myself with a yawn. I had something else on my mind, and it had kept me up all night. Only I wasn't sure how to say it, so I just blurted it out. "I don't think we should sit together on the bus."

"Why not?"

"Because some people think you're my boy-friend." I couldn't look him in his blue-gray eyes when I said it.

"That's just stupid," he answered so quickly, I felt a bit insulted. "Who thinks it?"

"Sage—and Maya, Ellie, and Anna, I guess. But don't say anything to them about it."

"Why didn't you just tell them we're best friends?"

I shrugged. I didn't mention that I'd told Sage he was just my neighbor. I was really ashamed of lying about it.

Gray scooped up a handful of gravel and began

throwing pieces at the school bus stop sign.

"You can sit with Raffi Tucker," I suggested. "The two of you could have a smelly sneaker smackdown."

"No thanks. I can find my own friend to sit with."

"Okay, we'll be secret friends. It will be fun!" My voice—all phony cheerful—made me blush. Gray didn't look convinced.

"For how long?" he asked.

"Um, I don't know." My stomach was beginning to feel like a squeezed-out sponge.

Suddenly he slung his backpack over his shoulder and crossed back to his side of the road.

"Wait! Where are you going?" I called.

"I don't think we should stand next to each other. It might look weird."

I knew he was right, so I stayed put. Even though he was just across the road, I felt lonely.

When the bus arrived, something even worse happened. Gray got on ahead of me and stopped beside Sage Green. "Can I sit with you?" he asked.

"Sure," she agreed, though she usually saved a seat for Maya.

I couldn't believe it!

"Sit down, Pixie," Mac, our bus driver, called.

I slid in next to Lucy Chang. In second grade

she and I had been in Brownies together. But I only belonged until it was time to sell cookies, because Mom hadn't approved. She said the cookies contained ingredients that were "heart attacks in waiting" and that she couldn't encourage our friends and neighbors to buy a single box. The troop leader said I didn't have to sell cookies. But I didn't want to be different from the other girls, so I'd quit.

"I'm saving this seat for Alexa," said Lucy. "But if you want, you can stay until she gets on."

Great. My ride was going to be like a game of musical chairs. "Okay," I agreed. "So what's up?"

She rolled her eyes under her straight black bangs. "Since second grade? You haven't spoken to me since then, Pixie."

"Sorry." I didn't feel like explaining I'd been too embarrassed to talk to anyone after the whole cookie thing.

But she seemed to accept my apology because she launched into a speech about her History Village Dolls. She had seven of them and she told me the name, birthdate, and exciting or tragic history of each one.

I listened and nodded, listened and nodded, until I felt like one of those bobblehead statues. The truth was, I'd always thought History Village Dolls were lame, even though they'd been so popular that in third grade, my grandma had given me Polly Pioneer instead of the hermit crab I'd really wanted. Now that we were in fifth, I couldn't believe Lucy still liked them.

When Alexa Pinkston got on the bus, I jumped right up. "Here, have a seat," I said as if I were a waitress at the diner. I looked around for another spot and saw Gray and Sage still chatting away. Sage was showing him photos of her puppy.

The nearest empty seat was next to a first grader. I sat down and took out *Ella Enchanted*, the book I was reading. It was a Cinderella-type story about a girl who didn't fit in with her family or at school, and whose only real friend was a boy who happened to be a prince. I felt so sorry for her, my eyes welled up.

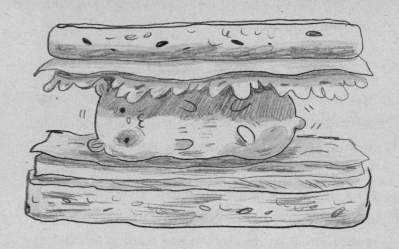

CHAPTER TEN
Ye olde Poetry Slam

When I got to my classroom, there was a message on the whiteboard:

Dear Girls and Boys,

 I am away at a conference today. Your substitute teacher, Ms. Doris Haggerty, will be helping you work on poetry writing. She is an expert, so please listen carefully. I want someone in our class to be Winged Bowl Elementary's first poet laureate!

Your teacher,
Ms. Tomassini

I stared at the woman sitting at Ms. Tomassini's desk. Instead of a black pointy hat and a cape, she was wearing black pants and a black sweater. And instead of a straw basket with a stuffed goose, there was a black, shopping bag–size purse on the floor beside her chair. But her frizzy red hair and the bandage on the side of her nose nearly made me faint.

I slunk down in my seat, hoping she wouldn't notice me, even though she was reading something on Ms. Tomassini's computer and didn't seem to notice anyone. For a while, anyway. Then she cracked her chewing gum a few times. I guess those whip-like snaps got everyone's attention because the room became quiet. Ms. Doris Haggerty, alias Mother Goose, smiled.

"Hi, kiddos. This is some classroom you've got." She lifted a paper off the desk. "It says here all I have to do is talk to the whiteboard and it will take notes for me." She wrinkled her brow as she read further. "Your teacher says I'm supposed to call it 'Stu' whenever I want it to write something." She didn't sound a thing like the fortune-teller at the Renaissance Faire. But like Mom had said, she'd been playing a role.

Lucy raised her hand. "Stu is short for Speech-to-Text Unit," she explained.

Ms. Haggerty cracked her gum again. "Thanks. I thought it was short for Stuart."

Some of my classmates laughed quietly, as if they weren't sure they were supposed to.

"Just kidding, kiddos," she said. "So I hear your school is having a contest for poet laureate. Ms. Tomassini wants us to practice this morning, by writing a poem in honor of Substitute Teacher Appreciation Day. Lucky for you, I happen to know about poetry."

"Oh man!" Raffi tossed his pencil on the floor.

"Blecch!" Chris Moran stuck a finger down his throat and gagged himself.

Gray surprised me by burping. He wasn't ever rude when Ms. Tomassini was around.

Ms. Haggerty raised a single eyebrow. "Is there a problem?"

Raffi waved an arm, but he didn't wait to be called on. "We can't write about substitute teachers."

"Why not?"

"Because Ms. Tomassini says we should write about the things we love. And no one loves substitutes. No one even likes you—I mean *them*."

"Well, I like poems that tell the truth. You can write about things you love or things you hate. But I also like poems that make me laugh." Ms. Haggerty turned toward the board. "Stu, write this down!" she ordered.

> "When we went to recess
> The class hamster vanished.
> I think the sub ate it.
> She said she was famished."

Ms. Haggerty smacked her lips and wiped her mouth as if she'd just eaten our class pet. Almost everyone laughed—then we turned to check that Sniffy and Whiskers were still in their cage.

Ms. Haggerty winked. "See how much fun poetry can be?"

Sage raised her hand. She wasn't laughing. "But that's not real poetry. Real poetry is supposed to express feelings."

"Hunger's a feeling," Raffi called out. It made me like him a little better.

Sage ignored him. "A poet laureate is supposed to write poems that have beauty and meaning. Yours is more like a Mother Goose rhyme."

"What about the poems Ms. Tomassini read us from *A Light in the Attic*?" Lucy said. "They're funny and the author, Shel Silverstein, is really famous."

"Right!" I hadn't meant to jump into the discussion, but there I was. "Besides, some Mother Goose rhymes have meanings. They're like a secret language or a message in code. My mother said 'Baa Baa Black Sheep' was a protest against unfair taxes. And that in 'Jack and Jill,' the woman called Old Dame Trot was one of the first woman doctors."

"Very good, kiddo." It was obvious Ms. Haggerty didn't recognize me, which was a big relief.

Sage whispered something across the aisle to Maya. Then Maya turned to me. "Since you're such an expert, could you please tell us what Ms. Haggerty's poem means, Pixie?"

I rolled my eyes as if it was the dumbest question I'd ever heard. "Obviously, it means she likes hamster sandwiches."

I was popular for the thirty seconds everyone spent laughing. Then Ms. Haggerty cracked her gum so loudly, it sounded like lightning had struck her teeth. "Okay, here's what I think is the most important thing about writing poems. They should be surprising. Whether it's because of the subject, the images you create, or the words you put together, surprise is the thing that creates magic."

Suddenly, I got what she meant—and what her hamster poem meant, too. It was about how having a substitute teacher in your classroom was a lot like coming home to find a substitute mom in your kitchen—a disturbingly weird experience.

I didn't volunteer to explain this to the class.

"Okay!" said Ms. Haggerty. "Now take out your writing notebooks and let's get to work."

CHAPTER ELEVEN
Ye olde Suspicious Sub

I couldn't concentrate on poetry. I was feeling desperate for an idea until I looked over at what Leo Glass, who sat across from me, was doing. Instead of writing, he was drawing. It wasn't the assignment, but Leo was like that. His picture of a lady monster with snaky red hair, tarantula earrings, vampire fangs, and a book that said POETRY poking out of her purse made me snort.

But if anyone heard me, I didn't notice. I had my idea. I was already working on my poem and everything around me had faded away. That's how I was whenever I was writing—a real-live zombie poet.

"Time's up!" Ms. Haggerty announced with a deafening gum crack. "Who's going to read first?"

Not me, not me, not me. I kept my head down and concentrated on making myself invisible.

"I will!" Sage volunteered. She grabbed her notebook and bounce-walked up front. Watching her sleek black hair swing across her back made me try to pat down my curls.

Sage flashed a big, toothpaste model's smile before she began reading. A lot of my classmates actually leaned forward in their seats. Including Gray.

"'Why We Need Substitute Teachers,' by Sage Green.

> "What would we do without substitutes?
> Stay home and rot our brains
> Watch TV shows and videos
> Play Xbox till our thumbs fall off
> Eat junk food till our stomachs ache
> And drive the adults nuts."

Everyone laughed and clapped.

"Nice job, kiddo," said Ms. Haggerty, which was as irritating as wearing an itchy sweater.

"It's free verse—it doesn't rhyme," said Sage.

"Yes—or have rhythm," Ms. Haggerty added. "Now who else would like to share?"

I leaned over my desk to block my notebook from prying eyes. Everyone seemed to think that anything Sage did was cool, including writing a poem. But it never worked that way for me.

A few painful seconds of silence went by. Then Sage turned around in her seat and smiled. "Since you're such an expert on poetry, why don't you read yours, Pixie?"

When she said the word "expert," her mouth puckered up like she'd just swallowed sour milk. I couldn't stand it. I grabbed Leo by the arm and stood up. "Leo and I did a poem and an illustration together. We'll both share," I said.

Leo's vampire-pale face turned paler, but he didn't say no.

"Thanks for coming up here with me," I whispered when we were in front of the class.

"I didn't exactly volunteer," Leo mumbled.

Ms. Haggerty cracked her gum again. I knew she meant we'd better shut up and start.

I elbowed Leo in the side and hissed, "Hold up your drawing!" Then I began to read:

"'Monster Sub,' by Pixie Piper
Is your substitute a werewolf,
a vampire, or a witch?
Does she have claws on the end of her paws
And a wart on her nose she can twitch?

"Does she make you write ridiculous
Rhymes in bloody, dark-red ink?
Then tell you to do each one again
'Cause she says your poems stink?!"

There were a few laughs, though no one clapped. As we walked back to our seats, I glanced at Sage. Her hands were folded in her lap, but when she caught my eye, she waved one in the air.

Ms. Haggerty nodded at her. "Do you have a question?"

"Um, I thought we were supposed to write a poem honoring substitutes. That poem was more like insulting them."

Well, you should know since you're such an expert on insults, I said in my head.

Ms. Haggerty sent Sage a doubtful look. "Insulting? Not at all! It gives me credit for having a lot of power." She looked around the room again. "Now, who else would like to read?"

"Wait! I have another question," Sage called out. "Don't you think free verse is much more artistic than rhyming poetry?"

Ms. Haggerty twitched her nose. "Look, kiddo, your poem was very creative. You used free verse to imagine what would happen in a world without substitute teachers. Instead of writing an essay, you were able to create images in our minds with a few well-chosen words."

Sage's face glowed like she'd swallowed a jar of lightning bugs.

"*However . . .*" Ms. Haggerty continued, "your friend's poem uses the image of a vampire teacher to let readers know what most kids think of substitutes. It's funny and honest, but it's also precise. The words in a rhyming poem have to fit just so in order for it to work. So I'd say the poems are different, but equally artistic."

Sage's glow became a glare.

But even though Ms. Haggerty's reply was satisfying, I kept my feelings off my face. Maybe now, the kids would start calling me Precise Pixie. At least it would be better than Princess Potty.

When it was time for lunch, I decided to eat with Gray. I figured since we hadn't sat together on the bus, we'd already proved we weren't tied to each other. Besides, he was the only one I'd mentioned the Mother Goose fortune-teller to. I couldn't wait to tell him who our substitute was.

But as I grabbed my lunch from the classroom fridge, I heard Ms. Haggerty say, "Pixie, would you come here for a moment?"

She knew my name after all.

I shuffled up to the front of the room. She was filing one of her scarlet nails. Soon the classroom was empty.

"Look, don't let that know-it-all discourage you," she said when she finally looked up. "You wrote a good poem."

I shrugged. "It was okay. How did you know my name?"

"I heard Miss Know-It-All say it."

I crossed my arms over my chest. "You heard it at the Renaissance Faire! I saw you there. You told my fortune, even though I didn't want one." Before she could say anything else, I began chanting:

"A rhyme in a pocket

A cinnamon curl

A secret uncovered

A Mother Goose Girl."

Her eyebrows jumped. "Oh, I remember you, now. I saw lots of bright orange in your aura. It means you're loaded with creative energy."

I knew she was trying to change the subject, but I wasn't going to let her. "That fortune is coming true," I said. "I'm even getting a goose—a real one, not like your stuffed bird. I found an egg near our pond and my dad made an incubator so it could hatch."

She blinked as if she were surprised. "So it was like the universe placed it there for you to find, huh?"

Suddenly I was pretty certain it wasn't *the universe* that had left Egg for me.

"Are you one of the Goose Ladies?" I burst out. "Because if you are, I want you to know I don't want to be one. I don't care if I'm a descendant or not. Tell the rest of them to leave me alone. I'm not joining you!"

The corners of her eyes turned down, and her jaw seemed to tighten up. I could tell I'd disappointed her. She might even have been angry.

"No one *has* to be a Goose Lady, kiddo. And even those who want to join aren't necessarily accepted. Just being born a descendant isn't enough. It takes courage and determination. Above all, you must be devoted to our mission. Not everyone is up to the challenge."

"What mission? Why would I need courage?"

"What does it matter? You've already made up your mind." She brushed some imaginary crumbs off her sweater. "I suppose you don't want a goose, either."

A little shock ran through me. Egg was practically the only thing keeping Gray and me friends right now. But there was more. Egg needed me. I wasn't giving up on it.

Ms. Haggerty glanced at the clock. "I'm going to lunch now. I suggest you do, too." She picked up her giant purse and walked out of the classroom without looking back, though I heard her mumble something. I think it was "Good riddance!"

CHAPTER TWELVE
Ye olde Gross Secret

When I'd come late to the lunchroom, I'd found Gray eating with Sage and her friends. So I'd joined the loners' table—kids who had their noses in books or just stared into space and didn't talk to one another. Maybe they'd had fights with their best friends, too—or maybe some of them didn't want friends. Not one of them seemed to notice when I sat down. But it hardly mattered. The surprise of discovering a real live Goose Lady in my classroom had made me unable to eat or talk much, anyway. The rest of the day wasn't much better. Ms. Haggerty allowed us to write poems about anything. Only there wasn't a thing I wanted to write about.

On the bus ride home, Gray sat with Sage again. I pretended not to see them as I walked up the aisle to the first empty seat—which happened to be next to Leo.

"Hi," I said.

He jerked his head at me, which I guess meant hello back. To show him I wasn't interested in talking either, I pulled out *Ella Enchanted*.

"What's that about?" he asked.

I tried not to act surprised. "It's like Cinderella and other fairy tales all mixed up," I said. "The main character, Ella, is under a curse that makes her obey anyone who gives her an order, no matter what it is. She needs to break the spell, but she's also got to deal with evil stepsisters, ogres, and other creatures."

"Does she have any special powers?" he asked.

"No superhero stuff, if that's what you mean. But she's awesome anyway. She's brave, smart—and she knows Gnomic and Ogrese."

"What are those?"

"Gnomic is the language gnomes speak and Ogrese is—"

"The language ogres speak," Leo finished. He

tapped the book's cover. "You know, this Ella kind of looks like you. Especially the cinnamon-colored hair."

My scalp got the prickles. No one had ever called my hair color cinnamon except for the Goose Lady. I looked at my book. Unlike the grouch I'd been seeing in the mirror lately, Ella's face was pleasant and smiling. And though her hair was the same color as mine, hers was straight and neat. Mine looked like the squiggles in a finger painting by a five-year-old.

"I never really noticed the cover," I said.

"I always pay attention to a book's cover. I want to illustrate books when I grow up."

Wow, he already knew what he wanted to do. I only knew what I didn't want to do. "You'd be great at it," I said.

"Thanks." He finally cracked a smile. "If you want, I could illustrate more of your poems."

"That would be cool—if I write any more of them."

"Why wouldn't you?"

"Because I don't want to be a poet or a poet laureate." My voice came out sharper than I'd meant it to.

Leo touched my arm lightly. "But you could still write them for fun. I'll never stop drawing, no matter what."

I knew he didn't mean to make me feel bad. It was

just that I used to think writing poems was fun, too.

I opened my book and began to read so I wouldn't have to think about losing poetry or Gray. But when we reached Sage's stop, I couldn't help but notice that Gray got off with her. He was the one who was getting to see the puppy. I hated watching him jump off the bus as if he couldn't wait.

By the time the bus arrived at my stop, I was feeling pretty low. I slipped into Acorn Cottage through the mudroom door and looked into the incubator. "I have bad news for you, Egg," I said. "Your pretend father is being a real jerk. I think he's forgotten all about you. He'd rather play with a puppy."

"Is that you, Pixie?" Mom called from the kitchen.

"Coming!" Gently, I turned Egg over and misted it. I even petted it a few times before I put the cover back on the tank. I'd agreed to take care of the egg and I wasn't going to back out. Besides, I was getting curious about the little bird inside.

Mom was sitting at the table, cutting something out of a piece of pink felt. "What is that?" I asked.

"What does it look like?"

"A dinosaur?"

She sighed. "It's supposed to be a poodle."

"Oh, I was going to say a poodlesaur." We both laughed.

"I'm making poodle skirts for my ladies," Mom explained. "I have to cut out twelve of these. Do you want to help?"

I went to the kitchen drawer to get another pair of scissors. "What's a poodle skirt?"

"A flared skirt with a poodle appliqué on it. We're putting on the play *Grease*. It's about teenagers in the nineteen fifties. In those days a lot of girls wore them."

"The old ladies are going to play teenagers?"

Her eyebrows rose up like gull wings in a stormy sky. I knew what she was going to say even before she uttered the words.

"Fun isn't just for kids, Pixie."

"I know, Mom. Sorry." My mother believed that no matter how old you were, it was important to have fun every day. I think it was because her childhood had been so full of rules and limits.

As I cut out the shape she'd traced onto the felt, I could feel her watching me. Lately it was something she did often, when she thought I wasn't looking. Probably she was wondering whether the Goose Ladies had come yet. I didn't mention Ms. Haggerty, though, because then I'd have to tell Mom I turned the Goose

Ladies down. She'd be so disappointed in me.

"Do you want to hear a secret?" she asked suddenly.

"Sure."

"Mr. Bottoms has purchased a new toilet for the museum. A really famous one."

"Whose?" I was hoping it belonged to a pop musician or a movie star.

"It's King Louis the fourteenth of France's throne toilet."

It was hard to get excited about a toilet that belonged to some old king I'd never heard of. But then I realized she'd said something strange. "What do you mean, *throne toilet*?"

The whites of Mom's eyes suddenly got big and she bit her lip to keep from laughing. "It's a throne with a potty under the seat. The king supposedly used it while he received visitors."

"E-e-ew! That's gross, Mom!"

She was giggling so hard her eyes teared up. "Mr. Bottoms is planning on having a big unveiling ceremony in a few weeks," she said when she could speak again. "But maybe he'll give you and Gray a sneak peek later."

"Gray went to Sage Green's house. I'll ask Uncle B. another time."

"Oh." There was a teeny bit of surprise in Mom's voice. I sort of wished she'd ask me when Gray and Sage had become friends. But then I'd have to admit the dumb things I'd said to Gray. Instead, I picked up the scissors and started cutting out another appliqué. With each snip, I imagined cutting off a lock of Sage's long, shiny hair.

"I'd better start dinner," Mom said when the last poodle was done. "Thanks for your help."

"That's okay. It was a lot more fun than doing homework," I said, lugging my backpack to my room. I had math, science, and two chapters of *The One and Only Ivan* to read. But first I pulled my poetry journal from the bottom of my pajama drawer and stroked the blue gray cover as if it were a beloved old cat. The I opened it and began to write.

> Gray is clouds, fog, and gloom
> It's worse than feeling blue
> Except when Gray is your friend
> Then the opposite is true!

Tomorrow I would try to make Gray my friend again. Once I told him about the throne toilet, he'd definitely want to see it. I was pretty sure none of Sage's seven bathrooms had one of those.

CHAPTER THIRTEEN
Ye olde Realization

Gray wasn't waiting at our stop the next morning or any other day that week. Only when the school bus had already pulled up did he run out his front door and get on. I guess he'd watched for it from behind the curtains in his living room, though I never spotted him doing it.

Even worse, he and Sage didn't just sit with each other—they were acting like best friends. I knew I'd have to eat lunch alone again, unless I got up the courage to ask Lucy and Alexa if I could sit at their table. So I did.

"It's not like we own it," Lucy answered, shrugging a little. "Anyone can sit here."

"Unless you're having a headcheese sandwich. Then no way!" Alexa said. "Even the name makes me nauseous."

"This is only turkey on whole wheat," I said, holding up my lunch bag. When I sat on the bench, I made sure to leave a little distance between us. At the end of the table, Leo looked up and sort of waved. He had a sandwich in one hand and a pencil in the other. His drawing pad was in front of him.

I was listening to Lucy and Alexa discuss whether headcheese was made from heads and if so, what kind, when Raffi came to our table. "Hey, Pixie, how come Gray dumped you?" he asked.

Alexa scowled at him. "Dumping is what you do to lunch leftovers, not people, Raffi."

"Besides, what makes you think Pixie didn't dump *him*?" Lucy added.

"We both got tired of each other," I said before they could argue anymore. "We've known each other since, like, kindergarten." It was nice of them to defend me—but I just wanted what had happened to go away. I wanted Raffi to go away, too.

Leo hadn't said a word while Raffi was bugging me. But when Raf was gone, Leo slid a drawing across the table. It showed a figure with a boy's head, a trash can for a body, and legs with sneakers that were giving off wavy "smell" lines. The boy's mouth was wide open and "garbage"—an apple core and a half-eaten chicken leg—seemed to be spewing out.

I showed it to Lucy and Alexa, and they cracked up. But after lunch, I stopped in the girls' bathroom to push the drawing through the swinging flap on the trash can in there. No one in our class really liked Raffi. He was the biggest boy in our grade, had a gray front tooth, and needed to use deodorant. Everyone called him Raffi Yucker instead of Raffi Tucker.

I didn't want to make his life any worse.

Without Gray, I didn't feel like exploring the woods. So when I got off the bus by myself on Friday, and Mom and Sammy weren't home yet, I went to the mudroom to hang out with Egg.

Sitting alone in its newspaper nest, Egg looked as lonesome as I felt. I considered giving it some company by surrounding it with chicken eggs from our fridge. But I was afraid they'd get cooked under the heat lamp, so I carried Egg outside and sat down cross-legged under a big oak tree.

I picked a few blades of grass and tickled the shell. I was thinking that when I'd told Ms. Haggerty I didn't want to be a Goose Lady, she hadn't even seemed to care. So why did I still feel bad? It was what I'd wanted, wasn't it? *To be free of the Goose Ladies.* Yet the surprising thing was, I missed the idea that they might come for me. I couldn't stop wondering about their mission. It was something that required courage. As Ms. Haggerty had said, "Not everyone is up to the challenge." I wondered if I could be.

Now that Ms. Tomassini was back, I'd never find out.

"I messed up, Egg," I murmured. "I was too much of a coward. I let you down. And Mom. And myself.

But maybe there was still hope. I'd returned *Sister Goose's Cautionary Verse for Brats* to Mom's shelf the morning after I'd taken it. Even though I'd only read the first poem, I still got the chills just thinking about it. But now I needed to take another look. I was hoping the book held a clue to how I could find the Goose Ladies, or at least *my* Goose Lady.

I took Egg with me to Mom and Dad's room. I had to remind myself the rhymes inside Sister Goose's book were made up, not true stories. When I felt calm enough, I pulled the book off the shelf. "Okay, Egg, I'll read aloud," I said as I flipped to the first verse.

"There was an old woman, who lived in a shoe.
When her brats misbehaved, she knew just
    what to do.
For dinner she fed them moldy old bread,
Then whipped them all soundly and sent
    them to bed."

I knew the rhyme well, but this version seemed meaner. Didn't the old woman ever hear of giving her brats a time-out? Couldn't she have grounded them or made them do extra chores, like scrubbing the floors of the "shoe"? Besides, in the illustration, the shoe house looked like an old, worn-out boot. It probably smelled like feet. Living inside it would be punishment enough for me.

But the next poem really made me want to puke:

"Trixie Piper picked a peck of pickled peppers.
A peck of pickled peppers Trixie Piper
    picked.
Then Trixie Piper ate the peck of pickled
    peppers
And retched because the peppers made her sick."

Yeow! It was bad enough that the Sinister Sisters, whoever they were, had changed Peter Piper to Trixie Piper—which was awfully close to Pixie Piper. But the illustration that went with the poem showed a stream of peppers exploding from the mouth of a curly-haired girl.

Super gross!

The poems in this book were creepy, but I turned the page anyway. It was like when you put on a horror movie that's too horrible—but you keep watching to see what happens.

> "Sing a song of sixpence,
> A pocket full of rye
> Four and twenty naughty boys
> Got baked in a pie.
> When the pie was steaming
> The brats began to shout
> 'We're sorry! We're sorry!'
> And then they all popped out."

In the illustration, the boys were bursting out of a piecrust. As they ran away, their clothes were smoking and their mouths were wide open, as if they were crying or screaming.

I slammed the book shut and shoved it back on Mom's shelf. Sister Goose's rhymes were only about the sickening punishments waiting for children who didn't behave. There weren't any clues to finding Ms. Haggerty in it.

"Oh, Egg, I think it's better I turned Ms. Haggerty down," I said, cradling it in my hands. "Let's just forget all about this crazy Goose Lady stuff."

CHAPTER FOURTEEN
Ye olde Aisle 6

I was getting a glass of water from the sink when
Mom got home.

"Sorry I'm late," she said. "We had a drama at
the residence. Mrs. Looper claimed Mrs. Pyle was
in her seat at the two o'clock movie, even though
there are no assigned seats in the rec room. They had
an argument that lasted an hour and—" Suddenly,
Mom stopped and looked at me. "How was your day,
honey?"

"Okay."

But she knew me too well to be fooled. "I guess you and Gray haven't made up yet, huh?" she asked.

I'd never told Mom why Gray didn't want to be my friend anymore. She was always kind to everyone. She'd never understand how I could have been so mean to him. I could hardly understand it myself. And I didn't know how to fix it.

"He doesn't want to make up," I said, sounding as if I'd swallowed a frog.

Mom walked up behind me and put her hands on my shoulders. "Don't worry, he will soon. He's just stretching. Around your age, that's what kids do. They explore who they are by trying out new people and new things."

Stretching was a word with a lot more hope in it than *dumping*. I imagined Sage pulling Gray's arm, elongating it like a rubber band. Maybe soon, it would snap back again—and Gray would snap back, too.

"Why don't you come grocery shopping with me?" Mom asked. "We can pick Sammy up from Grandma Westerly's on our way."

"Okay." I chugged down the rest of my water.

"Don't rush," Mom said. "I want to change out of this costume before we go."

I gave her a second look. I hadn't even noticed that she was wearing a poodle skirt and saddle shoes with fluffy white socks. The funny thing was, I wouldn't have cared one bit if she'd stayed in her costume.

We were waiting in the checkout line when Mom looked up from her shopping list. "Oh fudge! I forgot the peanut butter. Would you run and get a jar, Pix?"

"Sure." I wriggled through the maze of customers and carts, toward the aisle where they kept the nut butters and jellies. I knew the store as well as I knew the path through our woods.

I'd just located our brand when I heard a loud *craaack*! Out of the corner of my eye, I glanced down aisle six. There was one other shopper. I took in her frizzy red hair and the bandage on the side of her nose, and I gasped.

She looked up from placing a jar in the straw basket on her arm. "Do you need help reaching something, kiddo?"

"Ms. Haggerty! I—I didn't think I'd ever see you again," I stammered.

"I do need to eat, you know." She raised an eyebrow. "Did you want to see me?"

No! Yes! I wasn't sure. "Um, maybe," I mumbled.

"Well, if you're not certain, I'll finish my shopping." She turned to go.

"Wait! Please!"

She looked back over her shoulder.

"I—I think I might have made a mistake when I said I didn't want to join the Goose Ladies. I have questions I can't stop thinking about."

She turned and faced me again. I could tell she was waiting for me to say more. I squeezed my eyes shut so I could concentrate.

"Lately I've been feeling like a part of me is missing." I wasn't sure that made any sense, but when I opened my eyes again, Ms. Haggerty had set her basket down at her feet. She was staring at me, as if I were a book she was reading. I clutched the jar of peanut butter to my chest and forced myself to meet her gaze.

"Ask your questions kiddo," she said finally. "I'll tell you what I can."

I began with the thing I'd wondered about the most. "You said the Goose Ladies have a mission. What is it?"

She glanced around before she answered, "Our mission is to bring hope to the world."

The way she was grinning at me made her look like she belonged here with the nut butters. I think she was expecting me to jump up and down. But her answer sounded like the words to a cheesy song or the message in a Christmas card.

"How do you do that?" I asked.

"We bake birthday cakes that can make wishes come true."

It wasn't what I'd been expecting to hear. It wasn't mystical. "Oh— so you give cakes to needy people."

"Well . . . not exactly."

"Then I guess you sell them to raise money to help needy people."

Her eyes got all bugged out. "Oh no! We *never* sell them. We distribute them secretly. No one knows who gets them. Not even us."

I was pretty confused. "Do you mean you don't know whose wish you're granting?"

"Exactly."

"But wouldn't it be better to choose the people who need it most?"

She put a hand on her hip. "How would you know who is the most needy?"

"I'd know who *didn't* need a wish," I muttered, thinking of Sage.

Ms. Haggerty cracked her gum so sharply I winced. "Look, kiddo, hope is the belief that something good might happen. It keeps us going. And if everyone— rich or poor, healthy or sick, happy or sad—has an equal chance of having a wish come true, it keeps hope alive."

"But what about *bad* people?"

"A bad person might just be someone who needs a bit of good luck."

I kind of got it, but I was still a little disappointed. I'd been expecting the mission to be exciting and maybe even dangerous. Baking wasn't either of those things, though once I'd gotten a blister from a hot pan of brownies Mom and I had made.

As if she could read my mind, Ms. Haggerty began reciting a rhyme:

> "A birthday cake without a wish
> Is like an ocean minus fish.
> Pretty to look at, but deep inside
> It leaves you quite unsatisfied."

At first it seemed like such a simple rhyme. But the more I thought about it, the more I realized how important every birthday wish I'd ever made had felt, even though I had no idea if my wishes would come true. Maybe most people felt that way. At every party I'd ever been to, the most important part was when we gathered around the cake. Someone would light the candles, and while the birthday person was making a secret wish, we'd all be quiet. Then the kid or adult would blow out the candles and we'd clap, sing "Happy Birthday," and eat.

But a birthday cake that was guaranteed to *grant* a wish—well, that would be amazing!

"What goes into a wish-granting cake, anyway?" I asked.

"Sorry, kiddo," Ms. Haggerty said. "You'd have to become one of our Goose Girls, which is what we call our apprentices, in order to learn our secrets. And that's a job you'd have to earn. It wouldn't be easy."

Suddenly my heart stood at attention like a soldier.

"You'd have to be braver than brave," she continued. "You'd have to be truer than true. You'd have to keep everything about the Goose Ladies a secret."

I nodded and pretended to lock my lips, but Ms. Haggerty didn't crack a smile. "I'm serious, kiddo. If you tell someone—anyone—you could both be in real danger."

"But I could talk to my mom, right? She already knows a little because of her own mother."

Ms. Haggerty let out a long sigh. "I'm afraid not. The less she knows, the safer she'll be. As I said, becoming an apprentice isn't easy."

I felt bad for my mom. But I believed she'd want me to try anyway—though only if I wanted to.

Suddenly I remembered something. "Ms. Haggerty? Did you ever hear of a book called *Sister Goose's Cautionary Verse for Brats*?"

She blinked, as if she were startled. "How do you know about that book?"

"I found it on Mom's bookshelf. It belonged to her mother. I've read some of it, but it's super mean and scary."

"Listen, kiddo, that book is just a bunch of bad baloney. The Goose Ladies had nothing to do with it—absolutely nothing. It was purely the work of the Sinister Sisters!"

"The Sinister Sisters? Who're they?"

Ms. Haggerty's eyes narrowed angrily. "They're an unhappy branch of the family—but a distant one. You needn't concern yourself with them."

"Okay, then I want to join," I said.

"You're sure?"

I nodded. "When do I start?"

"How about right now?"

"Now?" I guess I was expecting some kind of test or task. "But what are the rules?"

"There aren't any rules to beginning, kiddo. You just do."

PHWEET! PHWEET! "Attention Pixie Piper! Attention Pixie Piper! Please meet your mother up front at the manager's office now!"

"Oh no, I forgot! Mom's waiting for me!"

The light in aisle six began flickering. "You'd better get going, kiddo," Ms. Haggerty said, hanging her basket on her arm. Something was happening to her. She looked fuzzy.

I rubbed my eyes. "Um, Ms. Haggerty? You're fading around the edges."

"Oh, well, yes. It's my power."

I looked at my arm, but it was still solid. "Is it going to happen to me?"

"I don't think so. Each of us gets our own distinct gift."

PHWEET! PHWEET! "Pixie Piper! Come to the front of the store now!"

Ms. Haggerty began fading faster. She was disappearing into thin air. "Wait! Please, Ms.

Haggerty—do you know what my power will be?"

"Sorry kiddo. You never know until your gift appears. Now, call me Aunt Doris. We're related, you know." She shooed me off with a blurry hand. "Go! Hurry!"

"Okay, Aunt Doris," I said, dashing down the aisle.

"Pixie, wait! I forgot something!"

When I spun around, she was gone. But I could still her voice in my ear, whispering, "I left out the most important thing of all—guard your goose!"

CHAPTER FIFTEEN
Ye olde Second chance

Over the weekend I thought about what I could do to help earn an apprenticeship with the Goose Ladies. I couldn't be braver than brave until I knew what to be scared of. I couldn't guard my goose before it was hatched, either. I could keep the Goose Ladies' secrets, but I hardly knew what they were yet. The one thing left was being truer than true.

I'd actually looked up the word *true*. It had a couple of meanings that everyone knows, such as "real" and "not a lie." But it also meant "loyal" or "faithful"—which was something I hadn't always been to Gray. But I was going to change that. From now on I was going to be a truer-than-true friend.

So instead of waiting at the bus stop by myself on Monday morning, I marched up to his front door and knocked. It seemed to take forever, but he finally opened it.

"Hey, Gray!" I said, all bright and cheerful.

He looked around, as if I might have meant some other Gray.

"Come on out. Please. I need to talk to you."

"Aren't you afraid someone will see us?"

"No!"

"Huh." He didn't move from the doorstep.

"Um, I think I overreacted, worrying about us being seen together," I began. "Forget what I said about us being secret friends. Okay? It was silly of me." I tried to laugh, but it sounded as if I were choking on gum.

"Huh." He grunted again. His sneaker dug at the doorstep.

When I'd told Gray I wanted to be secret friends, he might have gotten the idea that I didn't think he was smart, fun, nice, and all that. But I did think so! I also believed that once Egg hatched, I could trust him to help me guard my goose. The important thing was, I still thought Gray was special. I wanted him to think I was special, too.

"I'm really, really sorry, Gray," I burst out. "It was a dumb idea to be secret friends. I was being an idiot! Please forgive me and come outside. I've got something amazing to tell you."

He looked up and eyed me for a second. "I've got to get my backpack." He closed the door in my face.

I was waiting at the bus stop when he finally reappeared. He took his time crossing the road. "Okay, what's so amazing?"

"Uncle Bottoms got a new toilet for the museum. It's King Louis the fourteenth's throne toilet from France and it's over four hundred years old. There's going to be a big celebration when it goes on view, but my dad said we could get a sneak peek at it after school today." I was talking so quickly it was like someone had pushed my fast-forward button.

Gray squinted one eye, which meant he was considering. "A throne toilet? Sounds interesting. But I can't today."

"Why not?"

"Because I promised Sage I'd help teach Angel to sit and stay."

"But you go to her house every day!"

"So? She wants us to be *friends*." The way he emphasized the word *friends* made me remember what I'd told Sage on the phone—"Gray's just my neighbor." I would've given anything if I could just take it back.

We waited in silence until the school bus rattled down our road. When the doors opened, I let Gray climb the steps ahead of me. Midway up the aisle I could see Sage aiming her smile at him like a flashlight. He didn't glance at me again as he sat down next to her.

But later in class that morning, he passed me a note.

I can go with you to see the you-know-what later. Sage forgot she has a dentist appointment after school.

When I looked up, Sage was watching me. I smiled at her, but she turned away. I couldn't help hoping she had a cavity.

CHAPTER SIXTEEN
Ye olde King Louis

Fortunately, the Museum of Rare, Historical, and Unique Toilets wasn't shaped like one. It was a long, low building made of white bricks and surrounded by pine trees.

"Hey, uh, hi," I said when Gray met me at the entrance.

"Huh," he answered, or maybe it was "Uh."

We sounded like Stone Age people. Cave Boy and Cave Girl about to discover personal hygiene.

There was a single route through the museum. Once you stepped inside, you were on the path of Toilets Through the Ages. We'd been there so many times we could have led a tour with our eyes closed. Right near the door was a rough stone bench with four keyhole-shaped openings which "users" were supposed to sit over. The description on the wall behind it said it was a public toilet from ancient Greece. Whenever I passed it, I was grateful that I lived in modern times where public toilets were individual, with real seats and doors.

My favorite thing in the entire museum was a potty that was hidden inside a stack of oversized books. I always wondered if it had been in someone's personal library. The realistic-looking books were carved of wood, and the top half of the pile opened like the lid of a treasure chest to reveal a bowl in the middle. Whenever we passed it, Gray always said the same thing: "Look, Pix—books with a surprise ending!" But today he didn't say anything.

About halfway through toilet history, we found my dad and Uncle Bottoms. They were installing a deep red carpet between the globe toilet from Belgium (which Gray had always called the World of

Poop) and my second favorite, the elephant-shaped toilet from India.

"Hi, Uncle Bottoms, hi, Dad. Is this where you're going to put the King Louis?" I asked.

Uncle Bottoms stood up and wiped his wire-rimmed glasses on a red bandanna. He had crinkly black eyes, a belly like a teddy bear, and a very enthusiastic way of speaking. "Howdy, Pixie! Gray! Yes, this is the spot. We thought a red carpet would emphasize its royal history."

"Where is it?" Gray asked, looking around.

"It's in the community room. We're keeping it out of the public's view until the big ceremony. But you two can have a sneak peek if you like."

Dad put one arm around my shoulders and the other around Gray's. "I'm glad you both came to visit. Come on, let's take a look." I was pretty sure Mom had told him that Gray and I were having some sort of feud.

The community room was where special presentations were given. The King Louis throne toilet was already up on the stage, facing out as if it were waiting for an audience.

"That's it?" I blurted. As soon as I did, I wished I could take it back. I hadn't meant to hurt Uncle B.'s feelings. Only, I'd been expecting the fairy-tale kind of throne—big enough for a giant, with golden arms and legs and a seat made of plump red velvet. But the King Louis looked more like the kind of chair you'd find in a stuffy old dining room—except for the white porcelain bowl beneath its seat cover.

"The design on the back represents the grand royal coat of arms of the old Kingdom of France," Uncle Bottoms explained. "See the angels and those leaf-shaped thingies? They're made of real gold."

"I didn't know you could paint with gold," I said, giving it a second look.

"Did King Louis really use it while he was talking to people?" Gray asked. "I mean, for you-know-what?"

Uncle B.'s dimples appeared when he smiled. "Yes, he did. I suppose King Louis thought a throne with multiple uses was practical. Especially since back then, relieving oneself was a social event."

Suddenly Gray looked as happy as if he'd awakened to a snowstorm on a school day. "A social event? You mean the guests were party poopers, too?"

I clapped my hand over my mouth to stop from giggling. But Uncle Bottoms hooted like a crazed owl.

He was older than my dad, but he still had a sense of humor like a kid. Gray fell to his knees, quaking like he was going to die. He actually pounded the floor. I was glad to see a flash of the old Gray again. I wondered what Sage would have thought if she could see him now.

Finally he got up and wiped his eyes on his shirt. But he still wore a lopsided grin I recognized as his mischief face. "Do you mind if I ask one more question about the King Louis, Mr. B.?" he asked.

"Sure, go ahead."

"Did you try it out?"

Uncle Bottoms shook his head. "No, never. I treat all of the museum's toilets like the priceless treasures they truly are. The history of toilets is also the story of how hard humans have worked to improve world health and hygiene. And in many places around the world, they're still working on it." Uncle B. winked at us. "Besides, I think most of these antiques would be dreadfully uncomfortable to use."

Gray nodded, but I could tell he was disappointed.

"We'll unveil the King Louis shortly after I come back from my trip to the Netherlands," said Uncle Bottoms. "It's been a while since I've reviewed the bathrooms there. I'm planning to meet with an antiques dealer who says he has a potty shaped like a Dutch wooden shoe."

"Do you think you'll ever find one shaped like a sneaker?" Gray asked.

"It's possible. The world is full of surprises."

CHAPTER SEVENTEEN
Ye olde grand opening

"Is it okay if I come over to visit Egg now?" Gray asked when we were back outside.

"Sure." I walked a little ahead of him so he couldn't see how surprised I was. Suddenly breathing seemed easier. I was beginning to hope things between us would become normal again.

"Hi, Egg, it's me, your dad," Gray announced as he hung over the incubator. Then his forehead wrinkled up. "Hey, is that a hole?"

"Very funny."

"No really, look!"

I took a second glance—and a third. Though it was hardly bigger than a pinprick, there was a hole in the shell. "It must have happened while we were at the museum! I'm pretty sure it wasn't there when I got home from school," I said. "Wow!"

"What should we do?"

"Just wait, I guess. My dad said the baby has to peck its own way out. We're not supposed to help."

Scrrritch. Our mouths dropped open at the sound of a scratching noise as soft as pencil on paper. Egg was definitely trying to hatch.

"Maybe we should stay here and keep watch," Gray suggested. "If I get my books, we can do our homework on the floor."

"Okay."

Gray gave Egg a last look. "I'll be back in a few minutes. Don't let anything happen without me."

"You'd better hurry," I told him, though I was pretty sure that hatching took time. But through the window I could see him running, windmilling his arms as if he might suddenly lift off. It made me smile.

By dinnertime the pinhole in the shell had only gotten slightly bigger. Mom invited Gray to eat with us, so he wouldn't miss anything. Afterward we played Jenga on the mudroom floor until Sammy decided to "hep us." We ended up building towers for him to knock down.

But Egg was a slow hatcher. So slow that when it was time for Gray to go home, we still hadn't glimpsed a feather.

"Come back first thing tomorrow morning," I urged him.

"Okay!" On his way out, he held up two crossed fingers for luck and I did the same.

"Time for you to get ready for bed—tomorrow's a school day," said Mom when she and Dad found me on the mudroom floor. I'd been writing in my notebook, but I closed it and stood up.

"Why is Egg taking so long?" I asked them. "Do you think something's wrong?"

Dad's eyes met Mom's before they settled on mine. "The gosling might be too weak to make it," he said.

"No!"

Dad put an arm around me. "We've never done this before, Pix. Maybe we should have turned it more often or kept a fan nearby to circulate the air. We tried our best. Now it's up to the gosling."

I wondered if like me, he and Mom were thinking

of Skye, my brother who hadn't survived. He'd been born when I was five—too early, too small, and too fragile. Even though he'd only lived one hour and eight minutes, I still thought about what he'd be like if he'd had the chance to grow up.

When Mom had gotten pregnant again three years later, I'd been afraid. What if the same thing happened? But she'd told me we had to have hope. She'd said living without it would be like living without the sun or the stars. And then Sammy had been born, strong and healthy.

Sometimes, hoping took bravery. I kept that in mind as I got into bed with my notebook. Since I'd decided I wanted to be a Goose Girl, I'd started writing poetry again. I had a feeling that if I did get to be one, I was going to need rhyming more than ever. Besides, writing a poem always made me feel better. So, before I went to sleep, I finished the one I'd been working on:

> Hope is contagious,
> But not a disease.
> It won't make you cough, ache, itch,
> Upchuck, or sneeze.
> It's not like a yawn
> or a tune that you hum.

It's the feeling you're waiting
For good things to come.

"See you tomorrow, Egg," I whispered. But the idea of leaving the gosling all alone to hatch didn't seem right. So after I was sure my parents were asleep, I crept back to the mudroom.

The long, jagged line that ran along Egg's shell made me gasp. There were also small, squiggly cracks trailing off it in every direction. And when I leaned into the tank, I heard a wheezy little squeak.

"It's okay, Egg. I'm waiting here for you," I murmured. The shell rocked slightly, as if it were trying to answer. It reminded me of when Sammy was a tiny baby, learning to turn over in his crib. He'd seemed so helpless I'd wanted to give him a little push. Instead, I'd stood over him for a long time, rooting for him to do it himself. When he finally did, he cried because he'd gotten scared. But I'd been thrilled.

"Come on Egg, you can do it!" I whispered.

Egg managed another pitiful peep. It sounded like a cry for help, but Dad had warned me that picking off pieces of shell could injure the gosling—unless it was struggling for too long. Then it had to be helped or it would die.

But how long was too long?

For a while the crack seemed to stretch and shrink. Finally, it spread into an opening about the size of my pinky nail. I could see something! A beak or maybe a foot. Egg wobbled again and then was quiet.

"You must be exhausted, Egg. I am, too." My legs trembled in agreement. I grabbed a few clean towels from the stack above the washer and made a bed for myself on the floor.

Just before I lay down, I remembered the poem Mom had recited when she first told me about the Goose Ladies—the one she'd learned from her mother. I don't know why, but I thought it might help Egg. So, I leaned over the tank and whispered it:

> "Fragile, light, and sturdy
> To house a little birdie
> Or enclose a tiny sun
> Then it cracks—and hope's begun!"

I don't even remember falling asleep.

CHAPTER EIGHTEEN
Ye olde Destiny

When I awoke, the light through the window was as pale as the ginger tea Mom gave me for stomachaches. I rolled onto my back and stared at the cracks on the mudroom ceiling, which looked like the ones on Egg's shell. I studied them for a long time because I was afraid to look in the incubator. The room was so quiet. In the woods you couldn't help but run into dead animals sometimes—baby birds that had fallen out of the nest or half-eaten squirrels a hawk had dropped. But I couldn't face a broken shell and a limp gosling. Not yet.

I must have drifted off again, when I heard something. It was a wheezy squeak that pulled me out of sleep and onto my feet. There in the tank was a tiny, fragile, *live* bird! Its feathers were damp and it huddled under the heat lamp with a small piece of shell stuck on its back. Suddenly its bright eyes focused on me and it squeaked again.

That got me moving. I wrapped the little creature in a towel and dried it gently. Then I lifted it up to my cheek. Its down brushed against my skin so lightly, I could barely feel it. It was strange how something so soft could make me feel so fierce inside.

I was sitting on the floor with the gosling nestled in my lap when my parents came in. They were still wearing their pajamas. "I'll be darned, it looks like you've got an Embden there," Dad whispered when he saw us.

"What's an Embden?" I asked.

"It's the kind of goose you see in Mother Goose books," Mom answered. "You know, the ones with snow-white feathers, orange beaks and feet, and those bright blue eyes."

"It isn't really white—it's yellowish gray," I pointed out.

"That's just baby down. Its real feathers will come

in white," Dad said. He shook his head. "I wonder where that egg came from? I've only seen Canada geese around here."

"Maybe its mom stopped here on her way to somewhere else," I suggested.

Dad scratched his belly and yawned. "Not likely, honey. Embdens are domestic. They aren't good fliers like wild geese."

"Then it must have been magic." Mom grinned at Dad in a jokey way. Still, the word *magic* made the back of my neck prickle.

"May I?" Dad asked, taking the gosling from my hands. When he turned it upside down, the baby let out a tiny squeak of protest. "Aha, it's a female," he said as he examined it.

Mom clapped her hands. "A girl! What will you call her, Pix?"

"Oh, I don't think we should give her a name," said Dad quickly. "For all our sakes, we shouldn't get too close to this little one. It will only make it tougher to give her to a farm or a petting zoo."

"But I want to keep her!" I took the gosling back from Dad and tucked her between my chin and my neck.

My father tilted his head to one side as he looked

at me. "You'd better think carefully about it. She won't be a fluff ball for long. Like any pet, she'd be a responsibility. You'd have to feed her, clean up after her, and keep her safe."

I remembered Aunt Doris's last words to me, "Above all, guard your goose." But it wasn't the only reason I wanted to keep her. I knew I'd begun loving her before she even hatched.

I turned to Mom. "I think she was meant for me," I pleaded.

Mom's eyes, all big and moist, told me she understood. "It's your choice," she answered. Then she gazed at Dad with her chin tipped up in the air. I recognized that look. It meant she was standing her ground.

"I guess I'm outvoted." Dad reached out a finger and rubbed the gosling's head. "Welcome to the family, little . . ." He stopped and looked at me. "What are you going to call her?"

Before I could answer, there was a tap on the mudroom door. Dad opened it. Gray's sneakers were untied and his hair looked uncombed, but he was grinning like it was his birthday.

"Her name is Destiny," I announced as I placed her in his arms.

"Perfect," he whispered. "Hello, Destiny."

CHAPTER NINETEEN
Ye olde Greed

For the first couple of weeks she was with us, Destiny was all I could think about. I got up extra early, so I could spend time with her before school, and I ran home from the bus stop when I got back. I carried her around so much, Mom said, "That gosling will never learn to walk if you don't put her down once in a while."

"I don't hold her all the time," I replied. "When I do homework on the mudroom floor, she walks all over me. Besides, I have to share her a lot! I'm always letting Sammy hold her. Gray, too, when he comes over."

The truth was, I felt like a two-year-old with a new toy whenever I handed Des over to anyone, even my parents. I had to ball my hands into fists to stop them from acting grabby. I forced myself not to keep looking at the clock and sighing.

"I just think you need to have a few more human friends over before you start honking," my mother said.

I rolled my eyes and groaned. "Oh, Mom! I have friends—in school."

But that night, I brought my notebook into the mudroom and wrote a poem that wasn't about Destiny. It was about headcheese. Actually, I wrote three versions and they were all limericks:

> One
> The lunch ladies served us headcheese.
> I think it was made from pig sneeze.
> They said lunch I'd flunk
> Unless I ate that junk
> So I answered, "I'd rather fail, please!"
> Two
> The lunch ladies served us headcheese.
> I think it was made from pig sneeze.

In sliced bread they hid it
And when Sage Green bit it
She shouted, "I'd like some more, please!"
  Three
Some kids went on strike against headcheese.
They said it was made from a pig's sneeze.
But a cafeteria lady,
Whose name was Miss Sadie,
Said, "You'll eat whatever I please!"

I brought the poems to school with me the next morning. I wanted to invite Lucy and Alexa over to meet Destiny. We'd been sitting together at lunch every day since Gray had "dumped" me, and I'd given them daily reports on all the cute stuff Des did. But we'd never done anything together outside of school. I was nervous about asking them over. I was hoping the funny poems might make it a little easier.

"These are disgusting! I love them!" Alexa laughed when she read them.

"Yeah! Especially the one about Sage," agreed Lucy. "You should ask Leo to illustrate them."

"Maybe later." My face got so hot I could feel my freckles spreading like butter in a frying pan. Then the teacher on lunch duty blew her whistle. I needed to invite them before we had to leave.

"I, um, I wanted to ask you both if you'd like to come over and meet Destiny?"

"Are you kidding?" Lucy squeaked. "I thought you'd never ask."

They came on a Saturday when Destiny was officially three weeks old. As I led them into the mudroom, she began honking like crazy. "My dad says that a newly hatched goose thinks the first creature it sees is its mother," I explained. "So to Destiny, I'm Mom." I scooped her up and deposited her into Lucy's cupped hands. "Here—hold her close to your body so she'll feel secure."

I watched Lucy's black eyes grow shiny as she gazed down at Destiny. She didn't say a word, which for Lucy was very unusual. But I knew it was because there was no way to describe what it felt like to hold Des. She was so light, you almost weren't sure she was there. Yet she was so bright and alive you couldn't stop staring at her.

When it was Alexa's turn, Lucy pulled out a pile of miniature clothes from the tote bag she'd brought with her. There were old-timey dresses, hats, capes, and a fringed vest.

"Hey, aren't those for your History Village Dolls?" I asked.

"Yes, but I want Destiny to have them. I'm too old to play with dolls anymore."

"Come on, Lucy. That's just someone else's opinion," grumbled Alexa.

I twirled a prairie bonnet around my finger. "Whose opinion?"

"Sage's," Lucy admitted quietly.

"My mom collects dolls from all over the world and she's a grown-up and a judge," said Alexa. "She still has the doll that her great-grandma in South Africa made."

"Alexa's right," I agreed. "You should make your own decision." I felt bad that I'd sneered at Lucy's enthusiasm for her doll collection before I'd gotten to know her. I hated the idea that I could be as mean as Sage.

"I did make my own decision!" said Lucy. I could tell she and Alexa had discussed this before. She picked up a little red cowgirl hat and displayed it on her palm. "This one was Cassie Cowgirl's. Do you think I could take a picture of Destiny in it? It would make a super-cute photo for her baby album."

"Okay, but I don't have an album yet."

"Now you do." Alexa plucked a binder covered in baby bottle and teddy bear stickers from the bag. "It's from both of us."

"Thank you!" I popped the cowgirl hat on Dessie's little head. "Watch this!"

I played the old mix tape Mom listened to when she did laundry. The first song, "Girls Just Want to Have Fun," was Destiny's favorite. As soon as she heard the music, the gosling began swaying on her oversize orange feet, flapping her weenie wings, and waddling her backside. She looked like a windup toy.

I think the doorbell must have rung a few times before any of us heard it. "Oops! My mom must be back from the supermarket," I exclaimed. "She probably wants us to help her bring in the groceries."

We all ran to the door. But before I opened it, I peered through its small acorn-shaped window. A woman with a pointy face was standing on our doorstep. She had on a black jumpsuit and tall black boots, and in her wild, orangey hair, she was wearing a small straw hat that looked like a nest.

Suddenly she brought her beady black eyes right up to the glass. "I can see you, you know," she said in a voice that sounded like she'd swallowed a fistful of driveway gravel.

I jumped back.

"When her mom wasn't home, Penny Pioneer opened her cabin door and a bear was standing there," Lucy whispered. She was jumping up and down trying to see through the little window, which was too high for her.

"It's definitely not a bear," said Alexa, peering over my shoulder. "It's a woman with a bird's nest on her head."

The three of us started giggling.

"My mother is busy," I called through the door. "You'll have to come back."

"Your mother phoned me," the woman said. "I'm Raveneece Greed, the gosling rehabilitator. Didn't she mention me?"

Gosling rehabilitator? Were my parents trying to give Destiny away, after all? "Our gosling doesn't need rehabilitating. We're keeping her," I said.

"How nice," croaked the woman. "Well, as long as I'm here, I'll check it for the parovirus."

"Paro-what?"

"It's a goose disease—very dangerous. Since your egg was found in the wild, the chances are higher that your gosling is infected. If it has paro, it would need to be treated immediately. Otherwise . . ." She shook her head as if it were already too late.

"Um, can you wait? My mom will be back any minute." I turned to Alexa and Lucy with raised eyebrows.

"So she's not home!" The woman suddenly sounded cheerful. "Well, don't worry. I'll examine your gosling anyway."

"I can't let you in."

"That's all right, girlie, you can bring her outside. Your mother wouldn't mind that, would she?"

"Can't you wait just a little while longer?"

"Sorry. I have a long list of goslings to see today." She turned and started for the dusty blue minivan she'd parked in the driveway.

But I hadn't forgotten Aunt Doris's warning to guard my goose. I was pretty sure that included protecting Destiny from weird viruses.

"Pixie, don't!" Alexa warned when I reached for the doorknob, but I opened it anyway.

Raveneece Greed whirled around. "A wise decision, girlie. Now give her to me." She held out a hand. Her fingers were knobby and crooked. "I'll have to do the examination inside my mobile clinic. It will only take a few minutes."

"Um, okay," I said, stepping outside. But when I

tried to put Destiny in Raveneece's hands, she let out a hissing sound I hadn't heard her make before.

"Pipe down, Goose!" snapped Raveneece. Her gnarled fingers curled around Destiny's neck.

"She's just frightened," I said. I had to stop myself from grabbing Destiny back.

Raveneece turned a sharp eye on me. "Don't worry girlie, I know how to handle goslings. This will only take a minute." She slid the door to the minivan open and climbed inside. "You brats—I mean, girls—wait right there," she called over her shoulder.

Brats! I had a bad feeling before, but now I felt super suspicious. "Wait!" I shouted as the door of the minivan slid shut. In another moment, I heard the engine start.

Alexa grabbed my arm. "I think she's kidnapping Destiny!"

We ran toward the van and began battering the door—kicking, screaming, and pounding. For a second the van jerked as if it were stuck, then it took off with a powerful screech. We had to jump out of the way so the tires wouldn't run over our toes.

"Stop! Come back! Come back!" I shouted as we tore after the van. But the dust it kicked up created a cloud that made us stop in our tracks. Coughing and rubbing our eyes, we watched it vanish around a curve in the driveway.

That's when I began feeling really weird. Wind whooshed in my ears and words began swirling in my mind. Then a poem practically flew from my lips:

"Descendants of the Planet

In countries near or far

Please save my goose and set her loose

Stop Raveneece's car!"

A moment later, the sound of screeching brakes came echoing through the trees. I took off running, with Lucy and Alexa right behind me. As we came around the curve, we saw the minivan stopped—blocked by Mom's red SUV.

"Mom!" I screamed as she jumped out of her car. "The woman in that van has Destiny!"

Slowly the door to the "mobile clinic" opened and Raveneece stepped out. "You must be the mother of this lovely child." She held out a hand. "I'm Raveneece Greed, the Animal Welfare Department's chief goose rehabilitator."

"Where is Destiny?" Mom demanded, her hands balled at her sides.

"Is that what you've named the gosling? How sweet. She's safe and sound in my clinic, dear. Since you called me, I thought I'd stop and—"

"Called you? I did no such thing!"

"Oh? Perhaps I was given the wrong information. But what a lucky coincidence that you, too, have a gosling! With paro going around, I was going to give it a thorough examination at our rehabilitation center."

"You lied! You said you were going to check her in your van!" I shouted.

"I said no such thing, brat!" hissed Raveneece.

Moving as fast as a karate master, Mom pressed her cell phone into my hands and grabbed Raveneece by the arm. "Give us back our gosling right now or we're calling the police!" I hardly recognized my mother. She seemed taller and stronger than her usual self.

"Calm down, dear. This is just a small misunder-standing. Of course, you can have it back." Raveneece reached into her van and pulled out a canvas sack. When she turned it over, Destiny tumbled out.

I scooped her up.

"There!" said Raveneece, glaring at all of us. "Now if you'll move your car out of my way, I can go help someone who appreciates my services."

CHAPTER TWENTY
Ye olde Mysterious Me

"How'd you do it?" Alexa asked me as I locked us safely inside Acorn Cottage. Promising to be only a few minutes, Mom had gone to pick Sammy up from the Westerlys.

"Do what?"

"Stop that woman's van."

"I didn't."

"It looked like you did. You recited a mysterious rhyme and she stopped," Lucy said.

"Mysterious? That rhyme was *weird*." Alexa had

her arms crossed over her chest. I bet her mom, the judge, looked that way when she was about to send someone to jail.

"It was a coincidence! My mom came home at the right time. That's why she couldn't get away." I really hoped it was the truth and not some weird Goose Lady thing.

"Then who are the Descendants of the Planet?" Alexa asked.

"I don't know. It just came out. I was upset."

Lucy patted my arm. "Of course you were. We all were." She looked at Alexa. "Quit the courtroom stuff, Al. Pixie wouldn't lie to us."

Back in the mudroom, we settled Destiny into an old playpen Dad had dragged down from the attic after she'd outgrown the aquarium. It was lined with newspaper, which I changed every day. Des was only allowed into the rest of the house if she wore one of the special goose diapers Mom had made for her. But so far, she wouldn't keep one on for more than a few minutes without pulling it off.

When the door between the kitchen and the mudroom swung open, we all jumped. But it was only Mom. "Are you girls okay?" she asked.

"I guess so," I answered for all of us. "You came

home just in time, Mom. If your car hadn't blocked that woman's van, Destiny would be gone."

"I know. It was lucky."

"Do you think we should call the police, Mrs. Piper?" asked Alexa.

"Yes. I'll call and report it. Though my guess is that woman was probably just an animal-rights activist who got carried away with her mission. Anyway, I doubt she'll ever come here again. You girls were fierce."

"She wasn't just weird, Mom," I said. "She was scary."

From a storage shelf above the washer, Lucy grabbed a straw basket that had once held fruit. She balanced it on her head and croaked, "Don't worry, girlie. I know how to handle goslings!" It was a good imitation. We all burst out laughing. Even Destiny shook her head back and forth and honked.

"Can we have lunch now?" I asked, because there were questions I didn't want to think about, like how Raveneece Greed knew we had a gosling in the first place, and why we should believe she wouldn't come back.

In the kitchen we made food art by decorating open-faced peanut butter sandwiches with blueberries, raspberries, and sliced peaches. Sammy stuck his thumb through a slice of bread and called it "Daddy." Mom's sandwich was a smiley face with a peach slice for a mouth, but she only ate a small bite.

"I need to make some more poodle skirts this afternoon," she said. "I think I'll have enough material to make one for each of you, if you'd like."

"My mom thinks everyone is into costumes." I tried to make it sound like a joke. "Actually, she and the ladies at the senior residence are putting on the play *Grease*. It's about teenagers in the olden days."

"Right, the Stone Age." Mom sent me a sarcastic grin.

My stomach tightened as I watched Lucy's and Alexa's eyes meet. But then they burst out singing: "'We go to-ge-ther like rama lamma lamma ka dinga da ding dong'!"

"You've heard of *Grease*?"

"Are you kidding? Alexa and I always watch it when we have sleepovers," said Lucy. "We've memorized all the songs."

Alexa grinned and nodded. "You have such a fun job, Mrs. Piper. You get to do plays and wear costumes. My mother wears a boring black robe to court every day."

"I do love my job." Mom eyed me for a second. Then she turned to my friends. "Would you girls like to come to our Family Fun Fair?"

"It's no big deal," I added quickly. "The fair is run by a bunch of grannies."

"I'll go," said Lucy. "I love fairs and grannies. I hardly get to see mine since she moved to Florida."

"Well, my grandparents live five minutes away, but I'll go if there's bingo," Alexa said.

Mom put on a fake-sad look. "Sorry, no bingo. But we're planning lots of fun games. Ask your parents about it and tell them I'll drive."

CHAPTER TWENTY-ONE
Ye olde Hat of Horror

At bedtime I put Destiny into one of her diapers and smuggled her into my room. Mom said geese had dander, which is their version of dandruff, and she didn't like it getting on my bed. But I was worried. The lock on the mudroom door didn't seem strong enough anymore.

Destiny snuggled into the crook of my neck, as if I really were her mama. I could feel her tiny heart beating against my throat. We were both safe for now.

Mom tapped on my door. "Pixie? Are you too sleepy to talk?"

"No—but I couldn't leave Des downstairs. Please?"

"That's okay." Mom came in and sat on my bed. "You two have had a bad experience." She leaned down to kiss my head. Then she kissed Destiny's.

I realized she had a book with her. I recognized the worn brown cover right away. It was *Sister Goose's Cautionary Verse for Brats.* As if she'd felt my heart jump, Destiny fluttered her feathers.

"That book creeps me out, Mom."

"Have you read this one?"

"I found it on your shelf after you told me there was a book you'd hidden from your grandma," I confessed. "I'm sorry."

Mom stroked my forehead, as if she were trying to smooth out the wrinkles. "There's no need to apologize. I never tried to hide anything on my bookshelf from you."

"I only read a few pages, Mom. It's horrible!"

"I know. But I kept it because I thought it might be important someday. And after what happened this afternoon, I remembered a poem I'd read in it." She began flipping pages until she found what she was looking for. "Is it okay if I read it to you?"

I took a deep breath. *Braver than brave,* I reminded myself. Then I met her eyes and nodded.

She snuggled closer so I could read along:

"A hat is a hat
Except when it's not
It could be a basket
It could be a pot.
But beware of the hat
That was once birdie's bed.
Its wearer is evil
And birdie has fled."

A small black-and-white illustration beneath the poem showed a woman wearing a nest on her head. Around her feet were a few smashed eggshells. She didn't look like Raveneece—she was plump, with round cheeks, and she was wearing a frilly apron over a black dress. But the words seemed to be speaking right to me.

"Do you think it's about her, Mom? Raveneece Greed?" I asked.

"It can't be. I think this book must be hundreds of years old. I know it sounds weird, Pix, but I think it's a warning."

That gave me the shivers. Mom took my hand and braided her fingers through mine. "I think she's after Destiny," she continued. "That's why we should give her away. It would be safer for both of you. We could find a good farm—a happy place with other geese that—"

"No! Please, Mom!" I already loved Destiny as if she'd been mine forever. Besides, I hadn't forgotten the Goose Ladies' mission. I didn't know how it worked, but I was pretty sure Destiny was a part of it. And even though I was scared, I wanted to be a part of it, too.

Mom put a finger against my lips. "Shh, I won't make you. *For now.* But if I ever see that woman around here again, we'll have to find a new home for Destiny. It would be for her own good, too."

After Mom left, I took out my notebook. A poem was already on its way from my brain to my fingers and I could hardly write the words fast enough.

> I might seem peculiar,
> Except that I'm not
> It's just I'm a Goose Girl
> And moxie I've got.
> Don't mess with my goose
> Or misfortune you'll brew
> 'Cause I'm braver than brave
> And I'm truer than true!

CHAPTER TWENTY-TWO
Ye olde Unwanted Visitor

Monday was our class's day to work on the rooftop farm. The school's roof was covered with dirt-filled kiddie pools—the blue plastic kind—organized in rows. It wasn't as pretty as Mom's garden, but at least up here there was plenty of fresh air and sunshine. I plunged my spade into the soil—the dirt smelled surprisingly clean.

Lucy, Alexa, and I were crouched beside one another, planting tomato seedlings and talking about our new favorite subject. "You're not going to believe what happened last night," I told them. "When I tried to put the prairie bonnet on Destiny, she waddled away. But when I showed her the red cowgirl hat, she marched right to me."

"That's so funny!" Lucy exclaimed.

"What is?" It was Gray. He'd been planting with Sage and Maya a few pools over. We were friends again, but in school he still hardly ever spoke to me. So maybe we were secret friends.

"Destiny is," I replied without looking up.

Gray just stood there, poking the edge of the pool with a ratty sneaker. "Could I ask you something, Pix? Alone?"

Lucy and Alexa looked at each other and moved away.

"Okay—what?" I said.

Gray crouched down beside me. "She wants me to ask you if she can see Destiny."

"She who?" I knew perfectly well who, but I wanted to make him say it.

"Pix! Shh! Sage."

I rolled my eyes. "If you want to, you can show her Destiny's baby album on the bus later. It's in my backpack."

"No—in person. She wants to come to your house."

I wanted to act as if I didn't care, but I could feel my throat getting dry and tight. "She hasn't ever invited me to see Angel. Anyway, why doesn't Sage ask me herself?"

He shrugged. "I don't know. If you ask her over, she'll probably ask you back."

I knew it was useless to argue. "She can come if she wants," I said.

"Awesome!" Gray's face was shiny with happiness. It made me feel like socking him.

On Saturday morning I walked through our house, trying to see it as Sage might. Our round living room with its window seats was cool, but Sammy had recently crayoned one of the walls with his new favorite color, brown—which he called "chockit." Unfortunately the splotch on the wall looked more like something else. That reminded me that if Sage needed to use the bathroom, she'd discover we only had one. Like Lucy and Alexa, she might think the claw-foot tub was cool, but the pull-chain toilet was so old-fashioned, Uncle B. could have put it in his museum.

What made my heart hurt most, though, was the idea that Sage would be judging my room. There was so much I loved in it—the quilt Mom had sewn with patches of velvet, silk, and satin; the bookcase Dad had built and painted with peach-colored roses; and the lace curtains that had once been Mom's bridal veil.

Probably Sage would only see how tiny my room was. So small, I had to shut the door if I wanted to open my closet. Even my desk, which was in front of the window, was jammed in so tight, the drawers didn't open more than halfway without hitting my mattress.

As I straightened a pillow, I noticed my poetry notebook book sticking out from under it. I was stuffing it into my pajama drawer when I heard the doorbell. Smoothing down my hopeless hair one last time, I ran downstairs.

"Hi!" said Sage when I opened the door. She hugged me as if we were best friends.

I was so surprised I stepped on her foot. "Oof, sorry! Hi."

She looked down and smiled. "Is this your brother?"

I hadn't even realized he was beside me. "Yes, this is Sammy." Quickly I flicked a piece of macaroni out of his hair.

Sammy gazed up at Sage as if he'd been struck by Cupid's arrow. "Eat, guhl!" he commanded, holding out his mini box of raisins. He hadn't even offered me any yet.

"Thanks, Sammy." When she popped one in her mouth, his round face lit up.

With my brother following us, I led Sage on a tour of the cottage. "Everything here is so cozy and quaint," she said. I wasn't sure if "cozy and quaint" really meant dumpy and old-fashioned, or if I was just being oversensitive. Sage said almost everything with a smile.

Mom was just getting off the phone when we came into the kitchen. "Hello, Sage," she said.

"Hi, Mrs. Piper."

They'd met before because Sage's grandma lived at the senior residence.

"I haven't seen you around at Good Old Days in a while. I like your hair in that French braid."

"Thanks." Sage reached up and touched the back of her head. "My mom's been stopping to see Grandma on her way home from work, because it saves her time. So I haven't gotten to go, lately. Anyway, I've been busy training my new golden retriever puppy."

"That sounds like fun," said Mom.

"It is! Angel's the best."

I tugged the sleeve of Sage's sweater. "Come on, let's go see Destiny."

Sammy threw his arms around Sage's leg, but Mom unwrapped him. "Time for a nap, Sammy Wammy," she said, laughing. "Say bye-bye to the girls for now."

The mudroom wasn't as "quaint" as the rest of the house, but Sage didn't seem to notice. I lifted Destiny out of her playpen and we sat on the gray linoleum floor.

"You're acting just like Angel," Sage said when Des pulled at her shoelaces. She met my eyes for a moment. "I never thought a gosling and a golden retriever puppy would have anything in common."

"Actually, two things. They both like shoelaces and they're both adorable," I said, popping the red cowgirl hat on Destiny's head.

Sage stroked her soft back, which was becoming a mix of yellow down and new feathers. "Yes—but a goose is the perfect pet for you."

"Why?" I asked.

"Because she fits in with this house and your

family." Sage giggled. Des was tugging the end of her shiny braid.

"I think she could fit in a lot of places," I said. "I've read all about geese. They're very adaptable."

"Well, maybe. But Graham says my family is the golden retriever type."

"Why?" I asked, without looking at her.

Sage shrugged. "I guess, because we're more regular."

Suddenly I felt as spiky as a porcupine. "You mean *normal*?"

"Not exactly. It's just that your family is very, um, original? My mother would never let me have a wild animal as a pet. She doesn't even like dogs that much. Doesn't Destiny do her business in the house?"

"Doesn't your puppy?"

Sage blushed. "I try to clean it up before Mom comes home."

"Well, that's why I keep newspaper in Destiny's playpen. And I don't let her inside the rest of the house unless she wears a diaper."

Sage shrugged. "Nobody in my house would change a diaper."

"Then it's a good thing you don't have a baby brother."

"I guess so," said Sage, but she didn't sound like she meant it.

Okay, so I was a little sorry I'd said it. Maybe she hadn't meant to be insulting. Maybe she was just plain dumb.

"Let's walk down to the pond," I suggested. "There are all sorts of baby animals out this time of year."

Sage licked her lips. "You mean you're allowed to go there alone? I've never even been in the woods before. My mom freaks out if she sees a squirrel."

"Don't worry. Our woods are perfectly safe."

"Can we bring Destiny?"

I realized then that Des was magical—or at least, Sage seemed to be under her spell. "Sure, why not?"

"Can I carry her?" Sage asked.

"If she gets tired. For now, she'll follow us." I opened the mudroom door that led into the yard. "Come, Destiny!"

My gosling let out an excited honk. Still wearing her cowgirl hat, she waddled outside.

"Wow! I can't believe you already trained her to come," said Sage. "It took us forever to get Angel to do anything."

I shrugged as if it were nothing, though inside I was beaming. "I guess she's just as smart as a puppy."

CHAPTER TWENTY-THREE
Ye olde Malevolent Meeting

"Look, a downy woodpecker!" I pointed up at the plump, red-crowned bird that was drilling into a maple tree. "Isn't it pretty?"

But Sage didn't really seem interested in birds—or anything else in the woods. All she wanted to do was talk about "Graham."

"We play hide-and-seek with Angel all over the house. She loves Graham so much that when she finds him she yips and jumps all over him and bites his nose. And when Angel wouldn't bring back the tennis balls we threw for her, Graham stuffed one in his mouth to show her how it's done. He's so-o-o funny!"

"Let's talk about something else," I said when I couldn't stand it anymore. "I don't really care what Gray does."

"I know! I'm so glad, because I really like him. I used to think you liked him, too."

"I do," I said quietly.

"No, I mean *like* like," said Sage, with a sideways grin.

"Are you going to enter the poet laureate contest?" I asked to change the subject.

"Yes! I already chose the outfit I'm going to wear to the medal ceremony—I mean, if I win."

"Good luck. I hope you do."

"Really? Aren't you entering, too?"

"Uh-uh."

"Why not?"

I wasn't sure what to say. My reasons had changed. At first I figured that being a poet laureate would make me seem even weirder. Now it was because poems meant something else to me. I only liked writing them in my notebook, where they'd stay private.

"Look, wild strawberries!" I plucked two from a

cluster as red as jewels and popped one in my mouth. I held another out to her.

"How do you know they're not poisonous?" she asked.

"Because I eat them all the time and I'm still alive."

"Okay." She took the berry and dangled it over her mouth, as if she were daring herself to eat it. I shook my head and kept on walking.

"OH!"

I looked back just as Sage tripped over a root.

"Ow, ow!" Sage nearly landed on Destiny as she hit the ground. She grabbed at her ankle, which was stuck under the root. Startled, Destiny fluttered her wings. Then she waddled over to check out the grasses and shrubs.

"Are you okay?" I crouched down to help Sage untangle her foot.

"No, it hurts!"

"Let me see." I tugged at the root, but it wouldn't budge. "Maybe I should go get my dad."

"Wait! Don't leave me here."

"Okay, then you've got to try to wriggle it out. I'll push, too."

She nodded. It took a while, but we finally freed

her foot. When I helped pull her up, she let out a sharp gasp.

"Pixie!"

"I'm sorry!" I apologized again. It wasn't until I looked up that I realized she was pointing at something—a red fox. It was slinking through the brush where Destiny was exploring.

"NO! NO! Get away!" I screamed. I grabbed a stick and threw it, just missing the fox. It didn't act the least bit frightened—which was even more scary. It must've had rabies or something. Foxes were supposed to be shy—there was something wrong with this one.

But the fox wasn't interested in Sage or me, anyway. It was only after Destiny. My goose had never met a fox before, but when she saw this one she knew it was her enemy. She honked as loud as I'd ever heard her honk and fluttered her wings wildly. But she was still too little to fly.

Sage clutched my arm. "What should we do?"

"If it has rabies, it could attack us," I whispered. "But I've got to save Destiny."

"If I live, my mom's going to kill me!" Sage moaned.

Keeping one eye on the fox, I edged closer to Des. I tried to grab her, but she was so frightened, it was as if she didn't know me. When my fingers brushed her back, she sidestepped out of my reach. I knew if I didn't get her fast, she was going to be fox chow.

Without warning, the fox sprang. Its jaws opened over Destiny, ready to chomp her head off.

"NO!" I shrieked. "No-no-no-no-o-o-o!" I could have kicked the fox—and it could have bitten me. But for a moment, we just stared at each other. Then it turned back to Destiny, who seemed hypnotized by its golden eyes. Behind me, I could hear Sage sniffling.

SNAP! The fox's jaws closed.

"DESTINY!" I screamed.

But the fox only got the little red cowgirl hat. Des had teetered away just in time.

Suddenly I felt a great whooshing inside and words began whirling in my head. This time I knew a rhyme was coming and I shouted it as loud as I could:

> Laws of motion
> Your powers I seize.
> Until we are safe again
> Make this fox freeze!

"Sweet Tooth!" a gravelly voice cried. "Look what

you've done to her, brat!" My heart smashed against my ribs as Raveneece Greed rushed out from behind a tree.

Sage squealed when she saw her. "Who's that?"

I was too shocked to answer. Where had Raveneece come from, and what was she doing here?

The fox was frozen, but not like an ice sculpture. It was more like a creature in a museum exhibit that had been stuffed and mounted on a pedestal. The red hat was still in the fox's mouth and its front feet were raised as if it were about to pounce. But even though it wasn't moving, there was fierceness in its eyes. I didn't trust it at all.

I looked at Destiny. She was flapping and trembling, but she was alive. I snatched her up and backed away.

"Your fox was going to eat my gosling," I yelled. "I didn't touch it!"

"Nonsense! Sweet Tooth wouldn't hurt a fly." Raveneece Greed lifted the stiff fox in her arms. "Poor Sweetie," she crooned, rocking it back and forth.

"It's not our fault," Sage said. "We didn't do anything!"

"Besides, it's not dead," I added, although I wasn't

sure how I knew that. "And you shouldn't be here. This is private property."

Raveneece scowled at me. "We wildlife rehabilitators must go wherever there are creatures that need us."

"I don't believe you! I think you're hunting! That's why you brought that fox with you. You nearly scared us to death."

Raveneece studied me. "*You*, frightened? Ha! If you expect anyone to believe that, Goose Girl, you'd better learn to hide your powers."

Although the day was warm and sunny, I broke out in goose bumps. "I don't know what you're talking about! Your fox had a seizure. Maybe it has rabies."

"Pixie, look—it's waking up," cried Sage. "Let's go!"

She was right. The fox was stirring in Raveneece's arms.

I stared long and hard at Raveneece. I wanted her to know I wasn't backing down. "My father is the caretaker here. He can have you arrested for trespassing," I said. "Go away and don't come back."

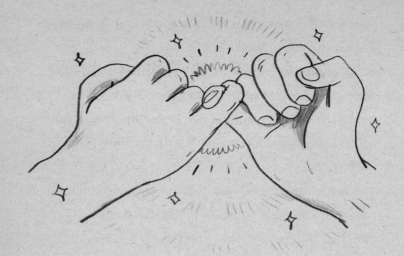

CHAPTER TWENTY-FOUR
Ye olde Secret Deal

Okay, so the fact that I'd stopped the fox was amazing. But it hadn't exactly been a surprise the way halting Raveneece's van had been. This time when the rhyme came to me, I'd understood it had power. Was this the "distinct gift" Aunt Doris had said I'd be getting? Oh, why did it have to be such a weird one?

I carried Destiny tightly in my arms as Sage and I half-walked, half-ran back to Acorn Cottage. Sage had seen what I'd done. She'd even heard Raveneece call me a Goose Girl. I wondered what she was thinking.

"That woman was really strange," I said to break the silence.

Sage burst into tears. "Ugh! How do you even know her?" she blubbered. "She looked like one of those wild people who live in the woods. I should have listened to my mom."

"But I don't know her," I said, surprised. "At least, not really. Once she stopped at our house by mistake."

"Well she seemed to know you." Sage swiped at her eyes, but she didn't slow down. "Or at least about your *powers*."

"Yeah—she really was a nut."

"Huh!" Sage huffed. "The fox didn't stop moving until you recited that rhyme, Pixie."

"The rhyme? It was nothing. When I'm nervous I start babbling." I smiled to show her I was back to normal.

She rolled her eyes. At least she'd stopped crying. If I were Sage I would've been suspicious, too.

When we approached the side of the cottage, we could see our mothers talking on the doorstep. Suddenly Sage jumped back and grabbed on to me. "Listen. Don't say anything about where we were or what happened. If my mom finds out I was in the woods, she'll ground me for years."

I hesitated a second before I agreed. "Fine. But, it would be better if you didn't mention what happened to that fox *to anyone*." I held out my little finger for a pinky swear and she hooked her own pinky around it.

But just as we were sealing the deal, war broke out between our mothers. We hid behind the hedge against the side of the house and listened.

"I hate to say this, Dana," said Sage's mother, her voice shrill, "but *Grease* is a poor choice for your theater group. It's undignified for senior citizens to act like teenagers. They'll just look silly."

"They won't look silly at all, Meredith," my mom argued back. "And your mother is doing a wonderful job in the role of Frenchy. You should come to a rehearsal and see for yourself."

"I don't need to see it!" Mrs. Green's voice was higher and louder than Mom's. "Frankly, I don't think the costumes you wear to the residence are very helpful, either. My mother is an adult—she doesn't need your childish games. She isn't going to be in your play and that's final!"

"That's so mean!" I started out from behind the bush to run to Mom's side, but Sage put a hand on my shoulder.

"Wait! We can't let them know we were listening."

I shrugged off her hand. For a few moments there was silence. When Mom finally spoke, her voice was calm but firm. "I think Gloria can decide for herself about being in the play. As you said, she's not a child. You can discuss it with her when you see her at the fun fair on Sunday."

Mrs. Green shook her head. "But I won't be there. I have more important things to do next weekend. Besides, I visit my mother on Thursdays."

"Are you sure, Meredith? The fun fair is an event that brings families together. The residents have been looking forward to it. They've put in a lot of work."

"I really must get going!" Sage's mom sounded impatient. "Where are the girls?"

Quickly Sage brushed the dirt off her knees and smoothed her hair. "Come on!" she whispered, hurrying around to the front of the house.

"Hi, Mom. Look how cute Pixie's goose is!" Sage chirped.

"What happened to your face! Did it bite you?"

I looked at Sage. There was a thin red line on her chin. She must have cut herself when she tripped.

"No!" Sage touched her face. "I guess I scratched it."

Mrs. Green raised an eyebrow in disbelief.

"Thank you for having me over, Mrs. Piper," said Sage.

"You're welcome here anytime." Mom smoothed down her poodle skirt and turned to Mrs. Green. "You know, Meredith, I have an idea. I'm taking Pixie and some of her friends to the fair on Sunday. Sage could come with us, if it would be more convenient for you."

I wondered how Mom could still be so nice after what Mrs. Green had said to her.

"Who else is going?" Sage asked, smiling at me.

"Lucy and Alexa." My answer made her smile shrink. Sometimes she could be such a snob.

"You forgot Gray," said my mom. "He's going with his grandma."

Sage cocked her head like a puppy. If she'd had a tail, she would have wagged it. "Can I please go, Mom? I'd like to see Grandma."

I started to worry that we'd oversold the fair. I mean, it was in an old people's home. The place smelled like bathroom deodorizer and overcooked veggies.

"Please don't whine," said Mrs. Green. "You know it gives me a headache." Poor Sage. I wouldn't have traded my poodle-skirted mother for hers, any day.

* * *

I was relieved when Sage and her mother finally drove off. I told Mom I was tired and went up to my room. I needed to be alone, so I could think about what had happened in the woods.

I flopped on my bed and squinted at the ceiling. "Aunt Doris, I'm worried," I said in case she was there, but invisible. "Raveneece Greed is definitely trying to steal Destiny. And I think I'm getting some weird power. It came out today right in front of this girl named Sage who's not even my friend."

Suddenly I heard a voice. "Pixie, is everything okay?" It wasn't Aunt Doris. It was Mom.

"Yes."

"Who are you talking to?"

"Um, the ceiling light?"

"Oh! Well, say hello for me," said Mom after a moment. "And dinner will be ready in a half hour."

"Okay." I listened to her footsteps retreating down the stairs. Then I turned my attention back to the ceiling. But Aunt Doris didn't show up or speak. The air in my room was just empty air. I began to wonder if I really was up to the challenge of becoming a Goose Girl, after all.

CHAPTER TWENTY-FIVE
Ye olde Not-so-Fun Faire

Instead of cooked cabbage and air freshener, the rec room at the senior residence smelled like fresh, buttered popcorn and cotton candy. Streamers and balloons hung from the ceiling, and there were game booths, craft centers, and snack tables everywhere. Mom had been working on decorations and stuff for the fair every night for weeks. I was really proud of her.

"Have fun, girls," she said, handing us long strips of tickets. I knew she'd be too busy assisting her senior ladies to pay much attention to us, but I didn't mind. It made me feel a bit like a teenager.

"That Flying Donuts game looks like fun," said Alexa. "You poke your head through the hole in that poster and try to catch one in your mouth."

"No way am I getting jelly and chocolate all over my face," said Sage. "Anyway, that's my grandma at the Paint a Mug booth. Let's go there." She headed off without waiting to see if we'd follow her.

I liked imagining Sage with donut smeared on her face. We followed her across the room anyway—even Alexa, who could be pretty bossy herself. Tiny Grandma Gloria pulled Sage into a long hug. She was wearing a navy tracksuit and a princess-like tiara. If her hair wasn't gray, I might've thought she was a kid.

Grandma Gloria hugged the rest of us, too. "I'm so happy you came," she said. "I hardly ever get to meet Sage's friends."

Classmates, not friends, I thought. But we all just smiled as if it were true.

Sage's grandma showed us the stencils we could use to design our mugs. The choices included animals, superheroes, sports equipment, flowers, and other stuff. I was about to choose a goose until Sage picked a golden retriever. I didn't want her to think

I was copying her. Instead, I found an acorn design I thought Mom would like.

"Graham! Over here!"

My paintbrush made a jagged line when Sage jumped up. Gray had just arrived with Grandma Westerly. Since Sage was already running to get him, I stayed put and picked out stencils he might like for his mug. After all, I was the one who knew him best. I selected two—a high-top sneaker like the ones he always wore and a wrench like my dad's. I didn't care what he chose, as long as he didn't use the same golden retriever Sage had picked.

But instead of coming back to Paint a Mug and her grandmother, Sage led Gray over to the cotton candy booth. Miserably, I watched the two of them stick little pink puffs to each other's noses and laugh.

"Ooh, she's so annoying!" whispered Lucy. "I don't mind that she dumped us for her grandmother, but now she's dumped her grandma for Gray."

"It's Pixie who should be mad," Alexa said. "Gray was her best friend until Sage stole him."

"Who cares?" I grumbled.

"Right! You've got us for best friends now." Lucy threw one arm around Alexa and the other around me.

Although the truth was, I did care that Gray was ignoring me, I was really grateful to have Lucy as a friend. And Alexa, too.

We finished painting our mugs and left them on a shelf to dry. "I'm sure Sage will come back to finish hers later," I told Grandma Gloria.

"It's all right," she said with a little shrug. "There are so many tempting things to do at our fair, I can't blame her for wanting to try them all."

I guess she was used to Sage being Sage. Still, I thought if I had a grandmother, I would have treated her better. My dad's mother had died while he was still in college. And my mom's mother had been killed in the crash. Sometimes I missed them even though I hadn't known them.

As if she could tell I was feeling sorry for myself, Alexa grabbed my arm. "C'mon, you need to have some fun. We can shoot out fake flames on candles with water guns at that booth over there. It's called Lights Out! I love that name."

"Okay." For just a second I glanced over at Sage and Gray, who were fishing with magnets on strings. They were laughing really hard as they tried to "catch" construction-paper fish with paper clips on them. I didn't see what was so funny.

At the Lights Out! booth, two ladies wearing plastic rain slickers, one yellow and the other pink, took our tickets.

"Here you go, girls," the pink lady said, handing over three water guns. She looked as big and comfy as an old armchair. When she grinned at me, I couldn't help smiling back. "You're Dana's daughter, Pixie, right?" she asked.

I nodded.

"I'm Kitty Beans."

I recognized her name right away. "I've met your sweater," I blurted.

"Your mom said you were a stitch," said Kitty, laughing. "Well, you're supposed to get three tries to hit the flame on the candle, but since you're family, you and your friends can each have six."

"Wow, thanks!" I said. But the candles were on a table that was really far away. Even if I had a hundred chances, I didn't think I'd ever hit a flame.

I pulled the trigger. A stream of water shot out of my gun, missing the candle by a mile. Lucy and Alexa didn't have any luck, either. Our aim was so bad we started giggling.

"Pixie, look!" Alexa called.

When I turned, water hit me in the face. "Hey!"

I shouted, but I cracked up and sprayed her back. Then we both turned to Lucy and got her, too. She doubled over, squealing.

"Other people are waiting, you know," said Sage from behind me. "Graham and I want a turn." I hadn't even seen them arrive.

"Okay, here." I spun around and squirted her.

Water dripped down her shocked face. I was shocked, too. I couldn't believe I'd done it.

"No fair, Pixie!" she yelled. "I'm wet!"

"Here, give that to me." Gray snatched the water gun out of my hand and started soaking me. So I grabbed Lucy's gun and fired back. We were both laughing.

Kitty Beans came hurrying over. "Kids, kids, stop! You're making a mess of the floor and the table, not to mention each other," she scolded. "Pixie, you don't want to upset your mother—she's worked so hard on this fair."

"Oops—sorry." Suddenly I felt like a wet rat. I'd been having so much fun I'd almost forgotten where I was. I glanced around the room.

"Lucky for you, your mom just ran to the supply closet. I think she missed this little flood." Kitty handed me a mop. "Here, clean up the floor right away before someone slips and breaks a hip. And you girls can dry up the table." She handed a roll of paper towels to Alexa and Lucy.

"You are such a loser," said Sage.

I gave her a wide-eyed, innocent look. "But you asked for a turn."

Gray burst out laughing. "Pixie's right."

"It's not funny, Graham!" Sage snapped. "Let's go." She pulled him away by the arm.

Alexa, Lucy, and I dried the floor and the table really carefully. After Kitty inspected it, she gave us a nod of approval. "Don't worry, I won't tell your mom," she said.

"Thank you," I whispered. I was so relieved I bit my lip to keep from tearing up.

Kitty patted my damp hair. "You girls didn't put out a candle, but why don't you each pick a prize from the treasure chest, anyway."

We dug through candy rings, mini cars, Super Balls, and other stuff. Lucy and Alexa chose glow-in-the-dark bracelets. I found a key chain with a tiny, goose-shaped flashlight that lit up when it was squeezed. It felt like good luck.

"Ick! I'm squishy," Lucy announced. "Let's go to the bathroom and dry off. We can use the hand dryer."

"Are you coming, Pixie?" Al asked.

"No thanks. I'll just hang out here until you come back." I didn't mention I'd just noticed a table I hadn't seen before. It was way in the farthest corner of the room, and its only decoration was a hand-lettered sign, too small to read. The fluorescent light above it was flickering in a creepy way. Yet something was drawing me to it like a paper clip to a magnet.

Whoosh! Snap! I was there.

When I read the sign on the table—PEANUT BUTTER WISH COOKIES, ONE PER TICKET—my throat started pulsing.

"Excuse me," I said as I eyeballed a plate of three nicely browned cookies. "Are those all you have left?"

The silver-haired woman behind the table was checking a sparkly cell phone. "Just a minute, kiddo," she said without looking up. That's when I knew.

"Aunt Doris!" I squealed. If the table hadn't been between us, I would have hugged her.

"Like it?" She patted her wig and smiled. "So tell me what's up."

For a moment I wasn't sure where to begin. Then everything that had happened came pouring out of me—Raveneece Greed showing up at our door, meeting her again in the woods with her fox, and reciting strange rhymes that seemed to have the power to stop bad things from happening. By the time I finished babbling, I was a wreck.

"You've done well," said Aunt Doris. But she sighed in a worried way. "I guess it's time I told you about your aunt Raveneece."

I staggered back as if she'd shoved me. "My what?"

She nodded and pulled out the chair beside her. "You'd better sit down. You don't look so good, kiddo."

CHAPTER TWENTY-SIX
Ye olde Horrid History

The moment I sat down beside Aunt Doris, things felt different. Our shadowy corner of the rec room seemed to get farther away from the rest of the noisy, bustling fair. The hum of voices laughing and shouting became softer, as if someone had turned down the sound. But most of all, *I* felt different. It was like I was floating above the room inside a soap bubble.

Then Aunt Doris cracked her gum, nearly giving me a heart attack. "Are you sure you want to know more about the family?" she asked.

"Yes," I whispered. "If I'm going to be an apprentice, I need to know everything."

"Maybe you're right, kiddo." She smoothed her cape and straightened her silver wig as if she were getting down to business. Then she began to chant:

> "Open up the mystery
> Of Mother Goose's history
> Where cakes and rhymes with hope unite
> And jealous sisters start to fight
> For cakes with power bring out greed
> In folks who want more than they need.
> As secret bakers we must strive
> To keep our Goosely quest alive!"

"But what does it mean?" I asked.

"Just that every family has its no-goodniks and that ours is no exception."

"You mean Raveneece?"

Aunt Doris raised an eyebrow. "Patience, kiddo. There's a lot to tell before we get to her."

I folded my hands in my lap and tried to look patient.

"Now, in the old days, everyone was a poet and rhymes were as common as bird chatter. Peddlers recited them to advertise their wares. Farmers bellowed them to call their herds. Shepherds sang them to bind new lambs to the flock. Cheese makers created them while waiting for their cheddars to ripen."

I grinned as I imagined a place where rhyming was almost like talking. "I think I would have liked the old days."

"Maybe—but it wasn't all fun." Aunt Doris shook her head and sighed. "Before Mother Goose began baking, she tried making her way as a poet. Even in a place where everyone was a rhymer, her verse stood out. Her rhymes could put babies to sleep and encourage rambunctious children to be good. They criticized unfair laws and ridiculed crooked rulers. But almost all of her rhymes made people laugh and raised their spirits. And in tough times, that was a lot. The townsfolk often gathered round as she planted her garden or tended her geese, just to hear her recite. Those who could afford it left her a few coins, though it was hardly enough to survive on."

"At least she had goose eggs to eat," I said.

"Right, kiddo. Though she had to sell most of the eggs in order to help support her sisters."

"Sisters?"

Aunt Doris put a finger to her lips. I rested my chin on my fist.

"One day a resourceful young printer came to

town," she continued. "He offered to put Mother Goose's rhymes in a book and share the profits with her. So she recited away—and he wrote them down."

"I guess she got rich," I interrupted. "Everyone knows her rhymes."

"Now they do, kiddo. But this was back when there weren't very many people who could read—or afford to buy a book just for entertainment. Mostly she gave them away."

"She must have been disappointed," I said.

"Well, perhaps. But there was one thing Mother Goose loved almost as much as rhyming." Aunt Doris winked at me. "She traded her last few books for flour, sugar, raisins, ginger, cinnamon, nutmeg— whatever tasty bits and bites she could find. Then she started a bakeshop in her woodshed. Before long, her cakes became known as the moistest, lightest, most scrumptious anywhere. People saved their pennies all year in order to buy one of her cakes for a special occasion. The fame of those cakes grew quickly. Soon they were in such demand, it became too much for her. And for Dandelion, her favorite goose, too."

"Dandelion's a cute name," I said. "But why would the goose care?"

Aunt Doris leaned close to my ear. "Because Dandy's eggs were one of Mother Goose's secret ingredients. Those eggs made the cakes light, receptive, and—"

"Wait," I interrupted again, "what do you mean by receptive?"

"I mean 'open'—in this case, open to magic."

"What magic?"

"Hold your horses, kiddo! I'm getting there."

I pulled on a pair of invisible horse reins, and we both grinned.

"To cut down on her workload, Mother Goose decided to bake cakes only for birthdays," said Aunt Doris. "At least her customers had those just once a year. Soon a strange thing began to happen. Everyone who got a cake from her had a birthday wish come true."

"How'd she do it?" I asked.

"Well, early each morning, she collected fresh goose eggs. Once she'd decided on the type of cakes she'd be baking that day, she foraged in her cupboard for the ingredients."

So far it sounded pretty ordinary. I must have sighed loudly, because Aunt Doris raised an eyebrow at me before she continued. "And when it was time for Mother Goose to mix her batter, she kept one hand over her heart."

"Oh." I pressed my left hand to my chest and used my right to mix an imaginary batter. Aunt Doris couldn't resist a smile. "Then what?" I asked. Her smile shrunk.

"Then she leaned over the bowl and whispered a rhyme into the batter."

"But what did she say?"

Aunt Doris cracked her gum. "Magic isn't magic if its secret isn't kept! Besides, you're not a Goose Lady yet."

"I bet the combination of Dandy's eggs and Mother Goose's rhymes made it happen," I mused, "like how accidentally spilling chocolate chips into cookie batter created the first chocolate chip cookies." I thought for a moment. "But didn't those wishing cakes attract even more customers?"

"You're right about that," Aunt Doris agreed. "Once people realized her cakes contained magic, Mother Goose's tiny bakeshop—which wasn't much more than a wood-burning oven, some bowls, and a slab of tree trunk for a table—was swamped with orders. People lied about their birthdays or the number of children they had in order to get extra cakes. They told their friends and relatives in other towns about the amazing cakes. Then it got worse. The greediest people—those who wished only for riches and power—began to scheme against Mother Goose."

"Did Mother Goose ever refuse to bake anyone a cake?" I asked.

"She tried, kiddo. But those crummy crooks began threatening her. The sheriff warned that he'd lock her in jail if she didn't sell him all her cakes. Thieves and thugs threatened to throw her in the river if she didn't turn over every crumb in the bakery. Then word of her wish-granting cakes reached King Cole himself, and he sent her an invitation:

YOU ARE HEREBY INVITED TO BECOME MY ROYAL BAKER
ARRIVE AT THE CASTLE, FORTHWITH
OR ...
BE LOCKED IN THE DUNGEON FOREVER AND A DAY
SEE YOU SOON!

"That wasn't an invitation, it was an order," I squawked.

"Yep. That's why Mother Goose closed up shop. She and Dandy disappeared just before King Cole's soldiers arrived for her. No one knew where she went."

"What happened? Did she keep on baking?"

Aunt Doris drew a line along the purple tablecloth

with her finger. "Unfortunately, that's where the trail of history grows as cold as old porridge."

"But what about her mission to keep hope alive? Why would anyone bother to wish if they didn't know they had a wishing cake?"

Aunt Doris smiled as if she'd been waiting for me to ask. "To this day, people still make wishes on birthday cakes, kiddo. Why do you suppose that is?"

I thought about my own birthdays. After we'd lost Skye, I'd wished for a baby brother each year until we finally got Sammy. Could it be I'd gotten a wishing cake? Then I realized it didn't matter.

"People make wishes because they have hope," I said, thinking aloud. "And when one wish comes true, it gives hope to others that theirs might, too. It's like a chain."

"And you, kiddo, are part of that chain," said Aunt Doris. "Many of Mother Goose's descendants are. There are groups of Goose Ladies all over the world, baking wishing rhymes into cakes and spreading hope."

"Isn't it amazing, though," I said as birthday memories filled my mind, "I always thought blowing out the candles was what made a wish come true. Everyone does! No one ever thinks the magic is in the cake."

"That's because as long as there have been cakes,

there've been candles, kiddo. To the ancients, candles represented the light of life. Some people believed their smoke carried wishes to the gods or kept evil spirits away from children. In their own way, they represent hope, too." Aunt Doris grinned at me. "And because people think blowing out the candles is what makes wishes come true, the magic in our cakes remains a secret."

That kind of bugged me. "Don't you or the other Goose Ladies ever wish people knew you'd made their dreams come true?"

"Oh no! Our lives are mostly peaceful these days. We're not the only ones who keep hope alive in the world, but it's enough to know we do our part."

As if she were done telling secrets, she opened her purse and fished inside. "Ta-da!" she said, whipping out her really red lipstick like she'd just done a magic trick. She began touching up her lips.

I was pretty sure she was trying to avoid telling me what I wanted to know about most. But I wasn't giving up. "What about Raveneece? You still haven't told me about her."

She shot me a sideways glance. "Are you sure you want to know?"

The question dropped into my gut like a rotten peanut, but I nodded yes anyway.

CHAPTER TWENTY-SEVEN
Ye olde Kid Sisters

Aunt Doris's next rhyme made me want to hide under the table.

"Open up the mystery
Of Mother Goose's history.
Four selfish girls behave like snakes
Demanding to have wishing cakes.
Their hearts are full of avarice
And in their minds is nastiness
But none expects to pay the price
Of acting not so very nice!"

"There are an awful lot of baddies in this story," I muttered.

Aunt Doris patted my hand. "Great gifts never come without problems. Unfortunately, Mother Goose had four problems—her kid sisters.

"When they were little, the girls would climb up on stools as their big sister worked, listening to her rhymes and—when they thought she wasn't look-ing—dipping their fingers in the batter. Of course, they'd make wishes as they licked them off. But Mother Goose didn't mind. Her sisters only wished for small things like kittens and seashells. She loved them so much, she never begrudged them those things."

I squirmed in my chair. I was thinking of all the time I'd been spending with Destiny and my new friends lately. "Mother Goose was a really nice big sister. I don't think I've been as good to Sammy."

"Maybe Mother Goose was too generous, kiddo. Maybe that's what spoiled them. As her sisters grew older, they grew greedier. They tried to convince her to give them entire cakes that they could trade at the market for the fine things they craved—leather boots, pearl earrings, legs of lamb, kegs of jam, fancy carriages, fine mares. . . . Oh, their list went on and on!"

"Pixie! Pixie! We've been looking all over for you!"

I glanced over my shoulder. Alexa and Lucy were waving from across the room.

"Oops, time for me to go, kiddo," Aunt Doris said when she saw them heading our way. The light above us flickered and she began to dissolve around the edges. "Here, take these to share with your friends." She nudged the plate of cookies toward me.

I stared at them for a moment. "But don't you have to distribute them randomly?"

"Cookies are just for fun, kiddo. Sometimes we make them with a touch of leftover cake batter to give them a wisp of magic." Aunt Doris winked at me.

"Thanks." I had so many more questions. Like if *Sister Goose's Cautionary Verse for Brats* had anything to do with Mother Goose's sisters—and if Raveneece was one of *their* descendants. But Aunt Doris was becoming fuzzy really fast.

"Take care, kiddo."

"Wait!" I yelped. "Where are you going? When will I see you again?"

"I've got to consult with the senior Goose Ladies. When I return, I'll be able to advise you. In the meantime, be brave. And don't let Raveneece near

Destiny. That gosling is one of Dandy's descendants!"

"I'll keep her safe, Aunt Doris," I promised. I wished I could hug her, but she'd become like a handful of glitter someone had tossed in the air. And then even that was gone.

"You're very powerful, Pixie Piper," her voice whispered in my ear. "Always remember that."

CHAPTER TWENTY-EIGHT
Ye olde Unhappy Ending

I ran over to meet my friends before they got to the cookie table.

"Sorry we took so long. The bathroom had a big line," said Lucy, crossing her eyes as if the wait had been painful.

"What did you do while we were gone?" Alexa asked.

"I got us the last of the peanut butter wish cookies from that table back there." I opened the purple napkin I'd folded over the cookies. "You have to make your wish before the first bite. And don't tell anyone what you wished for or it won't come true."

"Ha-ha!" Alexa said. But she and Lucy each took one and closed their eyes for a few seconds before taking a nibble.

"Yum, that was good." Alexa licked a fingertip.

"Yeah. Why aren't you eating yours?" Lucy mumbled through a mouthful of crumbs.

"I already had two while you were in the bathroom. I'm going to keep this one for Sammy." I folded the last cookie up in the napkin and shoved it in my pocket. I couldn't tell them I wanted to save it in case I needed a little extra luck.

"C'mon, let's try Ring the Bottle," said Alexa, hooking an arm through mine. Then she grabbed Lucy and led us off.

I let myself be pulled along, although what I really wanted to do was go home and check on Destiny. I didn't understand how Aunt Doris managed to be a secret Goose Lady inside and a regular person outside. (Well, sort of regular.)

Ring the Bottle had a long line, maybe because it looked easy. All you had to do was toss a ring around the neck of one of the old-fashioned soda bottles lined up on a table only a short distance away. Or maybe it was popular because the two ladies who were running it were making everyone laugh. A short, round one with a name tag that said SALLY was taking tickets. Every few minutes, she shouted:

"Three tries, three tries

Get one on and win a prize!"

Ginnie, the other woman, was in charge of giving out the rings. She gave each player a nickname like Sport, Champ, Ace, and Killer. When she called someone "Kiddo," I did a double take. But she wasn't looking at me.

"I just want to be called Next," said Alexa.

A sharp tapping sound made me turn around. Mrs. Green, Sage's mom, was marching across the room. The smile on her face was so tight it looked as if it had been sewn on. But I could hear anger in the clicking of her spiky heels as she headed toward the Paint a Mug booth.

Grandma Gloria opened her arms when she saw her. Sage's mom looked as if she were leaning in for a kiss. But I think she whispered something instead—something awful. Because Grandma Gloria's smile disappeared.

I spotted my mom leaving her post at the

ticket-selling booth and hurrying over to them. That's when I got off the line.

"Pixie!" Alexa called, but I was already running to Paint a Mug and I didn't stop. As I got closer, the voices became loud enough to hear:

"You're too old to be shaking your booty like some teenager, Mother! I insist that you give up the play."

"I can still make my own decisions, Meredith. Why can't you understand that I'm having fun?"

"Having fun doesn't have to mean acting ridiculous, Mother. I can't bear to watch you making a fool of yourself."

"Then please don't bother attending the play."

"Don't worry, I won't! And don't expect to see Sage there, either."

"Meredith, Gloria, please. Let's discuss this. I'm sure we can work it out," Mom said.

But Sage's mother stormed off toward the Pitch a Penny booth where Sage and Gray were standing side by side. Sage's fingers covered her mouth, and her eyes were wide and unblinking.

"Sage, we're leaving!" Mrs. Green snapped.

Then someone screamed. It was my mother. "Call an ambulance! I think Gloria is having a heart attack!"

Instantly the fun fair turned into a disaster like the kind I'd only seen on the news. An ambulance arrived. Emergency technicians and nurses surrounded Grandma Gloria before she was rolled out on a stretcher. Sage and her mother followed.

On the way home, my friends and I sat in the backseat of Mom's car. None of us were talking, although we were holding hands. I was trying to concentrate on hope—to write a poem about it. But I couldn't even think of a first line.

CHAPTER TWENTY-NINE
Ye olde Knockout

I was the last one into the kitchen the next morning. My poor mom looked panda-like, with big dark rings around her eyes. I guess she'd been up all night worrying. Dad stood behind her, rubbing her back in soothing circles.

"Did you hear anything about Sage's grandma yet?" I asked as I sat down for breakfast. Then I poured orange juice into my cereal. I guess I hadn't slept so well myself.

"Uh-oh," said Sammy.

"I called the hospital this morning, but they could only say that Gloria is still in intensive care," answered Mom.

Dad's slippers scuffed the floor as he went to get me a new bowl.

"That's okay, Daddy. I don't mind eating it this way." I was thinking intensive care meant Grandma Gloria was still alive. That was hopeful, wasn't it?

Before I left for school, I went into the mudroom to feed Destiny and change the newspapers in her pen. Dad and I had a joke that she was the best-read gosling in the world. I held her in my arms with her head under my chin. Her feathers felt as soft as breath on my neck. It was how we always said good-bye. But when I put her back in her pen, she honked in protest. She'd never done that before.

I turned on Mom's mix tape to cheer her up. I wished I could put the little red cowgirl hat on her, too. It always made her happy. But Sweet Tooth had probably eaten it. I hoped it gave that fox a stomachache.

"We'll play after school, Des," I promised her. "Stay safe while I'm gone."

Gray was sitting on the ground with his back against the bus stop signpost when I arrived. His knees were bent and he had his head in his arms.

"What's wrong?" I asked. "Are you sick?"

He looked at me with one squinty eye. "Sage called me in the middle of the night. We were on the phone for hours. She wouldn't let me hang up."

"It's awful about her grandma. She must've needed to talk." I swallowed before I added, "I guess you're her best friend."

"Sage did most of the talking. I finally told her I was too tired to say another word, but she said she just needed to hear someone breathing. I suggested she listen to Angel, but that made her mad."

"Why?"

Gray yawned. "When we first started sitting on the bus together, we talked about how we both wished we had brothers or sisters. We promised that if either of us ever got lonely, we'd keep each other company. She said I was breaking my promise."

I patted his uncombed hair. "Don't worry. Sage probably won't still be upset this morning."

He swatted my hand away. "I'd rather sit with you. Okay?"

"It would be mean, Gray. You'd be making her feel even worse. You should try to be extra nice today."

He dug the heels of his palms into his eyes and groaned.

I thought I might take my own advice and ask Sage to come over on Saturday. She'd probably love to play with Destiny and Sammy. A little part of me still hoped we might be friends, though I wasn't sure why.

But to tell the whole truth, there was another reason I wanted Gray to sit with Sage—I wanted to sit with Leo. Although I'd started riding with him because Gray was mad at me, I sat with him now because it was fun. Sometimes I made up a rhyme for a drawing he'd done in his sketch pad. Other times, he drew something to go along with a poem of mine. Then, last Friday, when I'd plopped down beside him, he couldn't look me in the eye. His knee jiggled so much his sketch pad bounced off his lap.

"What?" I'd asked, catching it.

He opened the pad and turned the pages until he came to a portrait of a girl's face. She had chocolate polka-dot eyes, freckles that looked splatter painted across her nose, and hair like the scraggly curls of a cocker spaniel. But the most noticeable thing was the scent that wafted off the page.

"It's me, isn't it?" I asked after a moment.

Leo nodded.

I leaned closer to the paper and sniffed. "Why does it smell like cinnamon?"

"I mixed some cinnamon spice with brown paint, so I could get your hair color right." He pointed to the half-smiling mouth. "You've actually got that look on your face right now—the one that means you're trying not to smile. I can't tell if it means you like it or if you think it's stupid."

"It's not stupid. I like how it smells—and I like the picture."

"Do you want it?"

I nodded, and he tore it off the pad really carefully. It was in my room now, taped high on my wall where Sammy couldn't reach. Every time I looked at it I felt tickly inside.

"You'd better get up," I told Gray as the bus turned onto our road. I reached down to help him, and he followed me up the steps. But as soon as we got on the bus, I could tell something was different. It was weirdly silent. I was careful not to look at anyone as I walked up the aisle. Still, I felt eyes poking at me, as if they were fingers.

Something stung my cheek. It was a silvery,

balled-up wrapper from a stick of gum. I looked around, but everyone was staring straight ahead.

Swoosh! A crushed-up tissue hit the back of my neck. Another got me in the cheek.

A murmur of quiet giggling began.

I forced myself to walk down the aisle, acting like I didn't notice.

Zing! A pencil bounced off my back.

The murmur turned into a chant. *"Stop it, Goose Girl! Stop it, Goose Girl! Stop it, Goose Girl!"*

"What's going on back there?" Mac called when I was almost to the empty seat next to Leo.

The voices quieted down. All except for one.

"Hey, Pixie!"

It was Raffi. He was my friend, wasn't he? I turned around.

Everything seemed to take place in slow motion. I saw Raf pull back his arm. I saw the ball in his hand. I understood what was about to happen—and for a second, I thought about trying to stop him. But if I did, everyone would see it. They'd hear my poem and they'd know it was true. So I just stood there.

CHAPTER THIRTY
Ye olde confession

I don't remember collapsing after the ball smashed into my face. But suddenly I was on the floor, staring up at the ceiling of the bus. For a few moments everything was blurry, as though I were underwater. Then, as things got more in focus, I could see that someone had stuck a wad of gum up there. I thought I saw Gray, but he disappeared quickly. Next Lucy's and Alexa's heads floated above me like balloons. The only sound I heard was my own moaning.

And then my dad appeared, so red-faced he must

have run up the driveway. He was big as a bear, but he carried me off the bus as gently as if I were a porcelain teacup. During the car ride to the doctor's, he sang one of his favorites, the John Lennon song "Beautiful Boy" to me. Only he changed the words to "beautiful girl."

Dr. Crow didn't think I had any broken bones, though she couldn't tell about my nose yet. She wanted me to stay home and rest for a few days while the swelling went down. She said I was getting a "shiner," which meant a black eye. There wasn't much to do for it except to use ice packs for my throbbing face. But if I got bad headaches or began vomiting, Dad would need to take me to the hospital for some tests. She said she'd call tomorrow to check on me.

Mom and Sammy were waiting for us at the door. As soon as he saw me, my brother burst into tears. "Peeksie boken!" he cried, pointing at my face.

"It's not so bad," Mom murmured. But when we passed the hall mirror she slipped a hand over my eyes and said, "Don't look!" Then she tucked me into bed with a bag of frozen peas wrapped in a kitchen towel to hold against my swelling cheek.

* * *

When I opened my eyes, it was four o'clock. I couldn't believe it! School had been over for an hour already. A few minutes later Mom cracked the door open. "Pixie, are you up? Ms. Mosely and Ms. Tomassini would like to talk to you."

The principal *and* my teacher! "Um, I don't feel so well. Can they call back tomorrow?"

"No."

"Can't you say I'm sleeping?"

"I'm afraid not, honey."

"But why?"

"Because they're here." Mom opened the door wider. Ms. Tomassini and Ms. Mosely looked in at me and smiled. The three of them squeezed into my room.

"Um, hi." I croaked.

"We're sorry to disturb you, Pixie," said Ms. Tomassini. She set a plate of chocolate chip cookies on my night table.

"Yes." Ms. Mosely studied my face. "You must be in a lot of pain. I hope these flowers cheer you up." She placed a bouquet of yellow daisies in a glass jar on my desk.

"Thank you." I smiled just a tiny bit because smiling made my face hurt.

"We'll only stay a few minutes," said Ms. Mosely, staring deep into my aching eyes. "It's very important I understand exactly what happened. Apparently someone told Raffi you could stop the ball with your mind." She raised her eyebrows. "Do you know anyone who would say such a thing?"

"No." I swiped at my cheek.

"I appreciate that you don't want to tattle. But this is very serious."

Without meaning to, I let out a weird snort-sob. "It was *me*. I told him."

My teacher and the principal looked at each other.

"Am I in trouble?" My voice came out so small I hardly recognized it.

"No, Pixie," Ms. Tomassini answered quickly. "But why would you say that to Raffi?"

"Yes, why?" Ms. Mosely didn't sound nearly as sympathetic.

I turned toward the window. "Because I was trying to be special."

Ms. Tomassini put a hand on my arm. "But you are special. You're a really kind person."

I think I caught Ms. Mosely rolling her eyes. "Well, it still wasn't right of Raffi to throw something at you," she said, "even if you did encourage him."

That felt unfair, but I couldn't tell her the truth. Miserably, I slipped down under my quilt. My principal and my teacher looked as if they didn't know what else to say to me now that I'd "confessed."

"I think Pixie is tired now. Maybe you could speak to her again in a few days," said Mom. Her voice was polite but firm.

"Of course," agreed Ms. Mosely.

Ms. Tomassini brightened. "While you're recovering at home, Pixie, you can work on the poem for the poet laureate contest. It's due on Friday. That should be fun, right? You're a wonderful poet."

"I—I don't know if I'll be better by then."

"That's okay—take your time. You can ask Gray to bring it in for you whenever it's ready."

CHAPTER THIRTY-ONE
Ye olde culprit

I stayed in bed for the rest of the day. Mom even brought Destiny into my room to keep me company. My gosling had learned that the reward for keeping her diaper on was getting out of jail (alias, the mud-room) so she didn't pull at it anymore. She still loved to dance to Mom's old mix tape, especially when "Manic Monday" came on. Actually, today had been the most manic Monday of my life. I didn't think I'd ever hear the song again without getting a headache.

On Tuesday morning Dad stayed home while

Mom dropped Sammy off with Gray's grandma and went to the senior center. When she and Sammy came back at two, they hurried straight up to my room.

"You're looking a little better, sweetie," Mom said. "Does your head hurt now?"

"Not too much." I always felt better when she was around.

"Oh, good." Her face relaxed into a smile. "I heard some news about Sage's grandmother. The nursing supervisor at the residence spoke to someone at the hospital. She says Gloria's heart attack was mild and that she'll probably be moved out of intensive care tomorrow."

"That's great, Mom." I wondered if Sage had though about how I was feeling. Yeah, right.

"Up!" my brother demanded, tugging on my quilt.

"Okay, Samster." Mom lifted him onto the bed. "But be gentle with Pixie."

Sammy was learning colors by studying the changes to my face. "Bu," he said, touching my cheek. "Yewwo," he added as he traced under my eye. When he kissed my cheek with his drooly lips, I got teary.

Later that afternoon, Lucy and Alexa called. Mom brought the phone into my room. "Just five minutes, girls. She's supposed to be resting," Mom told them before she handed it to me. I didn't even protest. It was hard to hold the phone near my face.

"We miss you! So does everyone in class!" they exclaimed. They were on the speakerphone at Alexa's house.

"Oh yeah? Then how come they were all throwing garbage at me?"

"It wasn't everyone, Pixie," Lucy said. "Just Sage and her idiot friends."

"Really?" In my fuzzy memory of what had happened on the bus, it had seemed as if everyone were against me.

"Yes, really," Alexa confirmed. "How's your face?"

"It hurts. My parents keep making me hold a frozen bag of peas on my cheek, but it doesn't actually feel that good."

"Victoria Victorian's mother put brown paper soaked in vinegar on her forehead when she had a headache," said Lucy.

"You want Pixie to take advice from a doll's mother?" asked Alexa.

"Every History Village doll comes with a book, Al!" Lucy told her. "I know a lot about what people in different historical times did."

"Maybe I'll ask my mom if we have any vinegar," I said, to stop them from arguing. "How was school today?"

"Terrible! Ms. Tomassini made us try writing a kind of poem called a haiku. Mine was the worst in the class," said Lucy.

"You always think you're bad at everything, but you're not. You're good at everything, Lu," I told her.

"Actually, mine was the worst," said Alexa.

If my head didn't hurt I would've rolled my eyes. "Tell me what else is going on."

"Well, Raffi's in real trouble," Alexa replied. "After your father carried you off the bus, he had a meltdown. He was screaming at Sage the whole way to school."

"What was he saying?"

"Let *me* tell," interrupted Lucy. She cleared her throat dramatically before she began shouting, "'You're a liar! A stinking liar! You told me she could stop things with her mind!'"

I wasn't that surprised Sage had told her friends my secret. But telling Raffi was different. Probably she'd pretended to like him, so she could get him to do whatever she wanted—like throw a ball at my face.

"Raffi will do anything to get attention," I said.

"True, but it made me think about the day that weird lady tried to kidnap Destiny," Alexa said. "Before she could get away, you said a poem. And her van stopped."

My heart started ticking faster. "That was just

a coincidence! My mom pulled in and blocked the van. You saw it. You were there."

"Okay, but why were Sage and her friends chanting, 'Stop it, Goose Girl'?"

"Because the day she came over, we ran into a fox in the woods. It was about to attack Destiny, so I screamed and it ran away. Anyone can scream, Al. It's not a secret power."

"What were you screaming?" Lucy asked. "Was it a poem?"

"I don't remember."

Lucy was silent. Alexa said, "Uh-huh."

I could tell they knew I wasn't telling the whole truth. I wish I could have told them that I was only trying to protect them. But it was a secret.

It was so quiet I thought they'd hung up. Then Lucy asked, "Are you okay, Pixie? We didn't mean to upset you."

"Yeah, sorry," Alexa said after a moment. I had a feeling Lucy had poked her.

"That's okay. I should probably go."

"Wait—there's one more thing!" said Lucy.

"What?"

"Leo asked us to tell you he hopes you get better soon!"

CHAPTER THIRTY-TWO
Ye olde Revenge Writing

On Wednesday morning Mom and Dad both went to work. Dad was only two minutes away in his barn workshop behind Uncle B.'s house. Still, he made me promise to keep the phone with me even in the bathroom, so I could call him if I needed him.

Actually, I'd woken up feeling much better. I even began working on Ms. Tomassini's poet laureate assignment. I was eager to do it because I'd had an idea. I wasn't even going to try to write a poem that could win. I was going to write one that would pay a certain person back for all the trouble she'd caused.

At noon Dad returned from his workshop to have lunch with me. While he made grilled cheese and bacon, I sat at the kitchen table and held a bag of frozen peas against my cheek.

"What did you do this morning?" Dad asked.

"Homework. I wrote a poem for a contest. The winner gets to be poet laureate of Winged Bowl."

"Sounds cool."

"Not really—it's just homework. Everyone has to do one."

"Can I hear it?"

"Okay." I put the peas back in the freezer and went to get the poem. I didn't mind. Dad loved everything I did—writing, drawing, and even singing, which I was truly terrible at.

He was flipping the sandwiches when I got back to the kitchen. The bacon-y smell was making my mouth water. "Okay, ready?"

"Yep," he said, waving the spatula.

"My poem is called 'Why a Goose Is Better Than a Golden Retriever.'"

"That's a goofy title."

"Daddy, shush!"

He pretended to zip his lips shut. I narrowed

my eyes at him and began reading.

    "My goose doesn't beg at the table

    She doesn't slobber or shed

    She doesn't chew shoes or eat up the news

    Or put muddy paws on my bed.

    "My goose never causes a problem.

    In her feathers you won't find a flea.

    She won't drool or bite, or howl in the night

    And on our good rug, she won't pee.

    "My goose is a pet that is faithful.

    In the night she won't leave you alone.

    Not like a golden retriever

    Who would dump you for an old bone!"

I looked up, expecting Dad to laugh, or even clap. Instead, he had a funny expression on his face.

"What's the matter?"

"I don't know. It doesn't sound like you."

"Why not?"

Dad ignored the question and asked one of his own. "Do you know anyone with a golden retriever?"

"Yes, a girl in my class."

"I bet she's not going to think it's very nice."

I scowled at the floor. "It's not supposed to be nice."

"I'm not going to tell you what to do because you know," he said as he brought our grilled cheeses to the table. "C'mon, let's eat."

I pulled out a chair and sat, imagining myself reading the poem in class while Sage's face grew red and teary. Suddenly my throat was so tight I had trouble swallowing.

"After lunch I've got to go into town to pick up a load of fencing," said Dad, interrupting my thoughts. "It should only take about half an hour. But Mom's going to be home late because Sammy's got an ear-ache and needs to see the pediatrician." He cocked his head at me. "Do you want me to ask Grandma Westerly to stay with you until one of us gets back?"

"That's okay, Dad. I can stay by myself for a little while. I'm not a baby anymore."

"You'll always be my baby," he teased. "You should try to nap anyway, okay?"

"Okay. I guess I'll do that now." I looked down at my half-eaten sandwich. "I'm pretty tired."

When he left, he was humming the same beauti-ful girl-boy song he'd sung when we'd been on our way to the hospital. I scooped Dessie up and went back to my room. My face hurt and now my heart hurt, too. I hated that I'd disappointed Dad. When

I got into bed I started to cry. Destiny got so upset she began honking.

After we'd both calmed down, she nestled atop my chest with her head tucked under my chin. She was getting big. I missed her babyness, but I loved the beautiful white feathers that were replacing her down.

I must have dozed off, because the next thing I knew, Destiny was making a big commotion. She'd gotten up on my desk and was looking out the window. She always honked up a storm when she saw a hawk or a fox outside, but I'd never heard her hiss before. She sounded as if she'd swallowed a cat.

"What's the matter, Dessie?" I asked quietly. "Did you see something scary?" I snatched the phone off my pillow and slunk over to the window, keeping out of view in case someone was looking up. I thought about calling Dad, but the yard was empty.

Still, Aunt Doris's last warning was flashing in my mind like a big neon sign: *DON'T LET RAVENEECE NEAR DESTINY!*

With my heart pounding in my ears, I hurried to my door and slammed it shut. Then, remembering what I'd seen on a TV show, I dragged my desk chair over and wedged it under the knob.

The doorbell rang. And rang and rang and rang.

Destiny began flapping her wings and honking. "It's okay, baby, let's go see who's there," I said, making my voice light and sweet. I yanked the chair from under the knob and opened the door slowly. Downstairs, the bell was still ringing.

With Des in my arms and the phone clamped under my neck, I crept downstairs. Secret or not, I promised myself I would call Dad, Mom, and 911 if it were Raveneece.

I held my breath as I peeked out the little acorn window.

It was Gray.

"What took so long?" he asked when I opened the door.

"Moving quickly makes my head hurt."

"Oh, sorry. But I think this will cheer you up." He held out the little red cowgirl hat.

Destiny honked and snatched it up in her beak.

"Where'd you find it?" My fingers shook as I settled it atop her head.

"It was right on your doorstep."

Gray and I locked eyes for a moment. Neither of us spoke, but I could tell we were wondering the exact same thing—*who left it there?*

CHAPTER THIRTY-THREE
Ye olde Revelation

I'd never expected to get Destiny's cowgirl hat back. I remembered how the fox had snapped it up in its jaws. It must have been angry when it missed chomping off Des's head—so angry, I'd figured it had torn the hat to shreds. But if I was right about who'd just left it on our front step, I knew I'd better worry about my own head. I grabbed on to the doorway for support.

"Are you okay, Pix? You don't look so good," said Gray. "Maybe we should go inside."

"I got hit in the face, remember?" I grumbled.

Actually, Gray didn't look so good himself. *"I know,"* he said in a choked voice. "I can't believe I didn't catch that ball before it hit you. I thought Raf was just fooling around. I didn't know he'd really do it."

"I know." I swallowed before I added, "I didn't think so, either."

"Yeah, but I found out something bad." Gray bounced his fists at his sides. "He did it because of this dumb thing Sage made up. She told him you'd be able to stop the ball with your mind."

"That was really mean. And stupid," I croaked. I felt guilty that I didn't tell Gray the truth, even though it was for his own good.

"Tomorrow I'm going to tell Sage she should apologize to you," said Gray. "Otherwise, I'm not going to be her friend."

I put a hand on his arm. "Don't—you might be sorry." I hadn't forgotten that I'd told him I wanted us to be secret friends. It was one of the worst mistakes I'd ever made. "So did you come to see my ugly face or to bring me more homework?

That made him crack a smile. "Oh yeah! I almost forgot—Ms. Tomassini asked me to pick up your poem."

I opened the door wider. "Come on in. I left it upstairs."

We climbed the staircase slowly. I'd left "Why a Goose Is Better Than a Golden Retriever" on my desk, and now there was the faint outline of a webbed footprint on it. I guess my floor was a little dusty. While I printed out a new one, Gray studied the drawing I'd taped onto the wall. "Did Leo do this?"

"Uh-huh. He gave it to me on the bus. Sometimes we do cartooning together. He draws and I write poems."

Gray grabbed a throw pillow from my bed and tossed it up and down. "I know. I've seen you," he said after a moment.

I hadn't thought he noticed anything I did anymore. I looked at my poem. I didn't feel like entering it in the contest. I didn't want to be mean anymore. "You know, this isn't really finished yet," I said. "Can you come back tomorrow?"

He flung the pillow up again. "I might be busy."

I was tired of trading hurt feelings back and forth with Gray. More than anything, I wanted it to stop. I wanted him to know that even if I had a dozen new friends, he was still special to me.

"Look, there's something you should know about me—something no one else knows."

"What?"

I pointed to my desk chair. "Have a seat. This will take a while."

I started at the beginning, when Mom had told me the Goose Ladies would come for me. Gray's eyes practically popped out of his head. I explained about meeting Aunt Doris—how she'd appeared as a fortune-telling Mother Goose, a substitute teacher in our own classroom, a grocery shopper, and a volunteer at the senior residence. I had to take a deep breath before I got to Raveneece. Just saying her name aloud made me shaky. But even when I told him what happened when Sage and I were in the woods, he didn't say a word. Or move. Or blink.

"So, do you think I'm crazy?" I asked, finally.

Gray stared at me, his eyes and mouth both wide open. I made myself return his look with a steady gaze. More than anything, I needed him to believe me. If he didn't, I wasn't sure I could keep on being brave or true anymore. Trying to be a Goose Girl was too lonely. No one knew what was in my heart.

As if she could read my feelings, Destiny began pulling on my sneaker lace. I scooped her up in my arms.

"Maybe I'm crazy, too," Gray said finally, "but I believe you."

I turned my face away until I was sure I wouldn't cry. "Thanks. It means a lot."

"So what are you going to do?"

I swallowed hard. "I don't know how to contact Aunt Doris or whether she's ever coming back. I just know I have to keep Raveneece away from Destiny."

"I'll help you," said Gray.

Those were exactly the words I needed to hear.

After dinner I sat on my bed, writing a poem for Lucy's birthday, which was coming up in a week. I was thinking of asking Leo to illustrate it when it was ready.

> If History Village made a doll
> That I could really talk to
> And if inside her plastic chest
> She had a heart that was true
> Then Lucy Chang should be her name
> 'Cause she'd be just like you—

"Pixie! Gray's on the phone," Mom called. "Don't move—I'm bringing it up." She was so nervous about my head, she'd hardly let me do anything but breathe this week. But I'd stopped arguing about it.

I felt guilty making her so worried.

"Thanks, Mom." I waited until she closed my door again before I asked, "Okay, what's up?"

"I can't stop thinking about your power," Gray whispered. "You stopped a car, Pix!"

"*I know*, Gray. I said a rhyme and the minivan stopped. But it was my mom's car that actually blocked it, so I'm not positive—"

"Right—" he said impatiently. "And you also stopped a fox from eating Destiny."

I sighed loudly. "It looked as if it was frozen, though it only lasted a few minutes. Why?"

"Because if Raveneece comes back to steal Destiny, you could freeze *her*. Then we could tie her up and call the police." He made it sound so simple.

"But I don't know if I could stop an actual person. I don't even know if I can stop *anything* again. Since the softball hit me, it all seems kind of fuzzy. What if I tried to stop Raveneece and it didn't work? That would be dangerous."

"That's why you should test your power out on me!" Gray said. "I don't mind." He seemed pretty excited about the idea.

It did sound like fun—unless something went wrong. "I guess we could try in the woods or somewhere else where no one can see us," I said finally. "But right now I'm not allowed outside. We can try it after I go back to school."

Gray was silent for a moment. "Raveneece has already been at your doorstep, Pix. I think we need to know sooner. I'll help you—tomorrow morning."

"But you'll be in school! Anyway, Dad only leaves me alone for a little while in the morning to go to his workshop. And in the afternoon, Mom watches me so closely, she can see me blink."

"I'll stay home. I can tell my grandma I'm sick."

"Ha! She's not going to let you out if you're sick."

"Tomorrow's Thursday, her shopping day. She always takes Sammy with her to the grocery store. Then they stop at the library. I can come over as soon as your dad leaves for his workshop. It's perfect, Pix."

Hmm, not perfect, I thought. But if I could actually freeze Gray for a few minutes, I might be able to freeze anyone—even Raveneece.

"Okay," I agreed.

"Wow, great!" said Gray. "I've already got the experiments planned. See you tomorrow."

CHAPTER THIRTY-FOUR
Ye olde Hermie and other Experiments

After Dad left for his workshop the next morning, I got out of my PJs and pulled on jeans and a shirt. Five minutes later Gray showed up carrying a crumpled brown grocery bag with him.

"What's in there?" I asked.

He was smiling with his mouth closed, and his eyes were all twinkly. "I'll show you when we get outside."

We went to our clubhouse at the back of the yard, which was really just a small grove of pines that felt private.

"Okay, now tell me," I said.

"I brought equipment for our experiments," Gray answered, unrolling the top of the bag.

"What equipment?"

He pulled each item out as if it were a rabbit from a magician's top hat. "This is one of Gran's individual serving size cans of tomato juice . . . this is my dad's old stopwatch . . . and"—he stopped to set down the first two things before he reached in and pulled out a jar with some mud at the bottom—"say hello to Hermie the wormie!"

I waved a pinky at the wriggling, brownish pink worm. "What kind of experiment is this, Gray?"

"It's three experiments, actually," he replied. "We'll start with the easiest and build up to the hardest."

I looked around. "We'd better get started. My dad won't be away for very long."

"Okay. Get on your knees while I open this tomato juice. I'm going to pour it on top of your head unless you can stop me."

I narrowed my eyes at him. "Why don't you pour it on your own head?"

"Because it's more likely to work if you're the one facing the consequences. Besides, you're going to stop me before you get wet, right?"

I had to admit he was making sense—but it still made me mad. "Well, okay," I said. "But why do you have that worm?"

Gray lifted the jar. "Hermie's going to help me test your stopping power, too. I'm going to drop him down your back—unless you freeze him on my palm first."

"You think I'm going to let you drop a worm under my shirt?"

"Hermie can't help it if he's slimy, Pix," said Gray cheerfully. "Anyway, he's only a couple of inches long. It should be easy for you to freeze him."

I crossed my arms over my chest and glared. "What about the stopwatch?" I asked.

Gray snatched it off the grass. "I think you'll like this one. I'm going to run around and around your house until you freeze me. As soon as it happens, you have to press the watch's Stop button. That way, we'll know how much time it takes to freeze a moving person and how long they stay that way. Doesn't that sound useful?" He grinned proudly at me.

I shrugged a shoulder. "I guess so."

"Good. Let's get started." Gray grabbed the tomato juice can. "Get down on your knees so I can reach the top of your head."

"Don't pour it until I think of a rhyme," I said, kneeling down.

Gray's face became serious. "In real life, your power needs to work fast, Pix. So hurry up and rhyme."

"Oh, shut up," I said.

Gray popped the tab on the tomato juice can. I put my hands over my ears, squeezed my eyes shut, and chanted.

"Mother Goose, Mother Goose,

Help me turn my power loose

Let's stop Gran's tomato juice!"

I felt the thick juice trickle through my hair and down my scalp. It oozed onto my forehead and behind my ears.

"Yeeuck!" I squealed. "It's dripping down my neck. I need a tissue or something."

Gray stuck his hand in the bag and felt around. "I think there's a paper towel in here," he said.

"Come on, it's running down my back!"

"Maybe Hermie will lick it up," said Gray. He thought for a moment. "Do worms actually have tongues?"

I lunged for the bag, but Gray swung it away.

"Ah, here it is!" He finally pulled out a paper towel

and handed it to me. "Why didn't the rhyme work, Pix?"

When I'd stopped the car and the fox, I'd gotten a scary feeling. It was something like having a tornado in my head. The tornado was made of words and it spun like crazy. It wasn't something I could control.

But it felt too weird to talk about, even to Gray. "I'm not sure," I said. "It could be the rhyme wasn't good enough."

"Let's try Hermie next," Gray said. "Maybe you'll have more luck."

I stared him in the eyes. I wasn't grossed out by spiders, stinkbugs, or worms. But Gray seemed to be having too much fun with this. "If I freeze him on your palm, you won't put him down my back, right?" I asked.

"O-o-okay," said Gray, grudgingly. He poured Hermie out into his palm and walked behind me. With a finger he pulled my shirt away from my neck.

"Rhyme!" he demanded.

I stood quietly and listened to my own breath as I waited for the word tornado. But all I felt was Gray pulling the neck of my T-shirt out farther. A rhyme appeared in my head and I hurried to recite it:

Hermie Wormie on Gray's palm

While I freeze you, please stay calm.

Time will stop, but it won't hurt

And you will stay out of my shirt!

"There, I did it!" I shouted. Right?"

The next thing I knew, a wriggling Hermie wiggled down my back. "Ew!" I squawked, pulling out the bottom of my shirt. I whirled around as Hermie landed in the grass.

"Bye, Hermie!" said Gray as the earthworm slithered away. "You were a really great performer."

"Ha-ha. That wasn't funny," I snapped.

But Gray wasn't grinning. "Maybe you're not trying hard enough." He placed the stopwatch in my hand. "Pretend I'm Raveneece running around your house. She's looking for a way in. You've got to stop her."

"Okay," I agreed. I pressed the timer button and Gray took off. Right away, a rhyme appeared in my mind:

Bone and muscle hear my call

Legs will stiffen, boy will fall.

Still as stone in grass he lies

No one hears his silent cries.

The rhyme seemed scary, even to me. But I was

desperate to make one that worked. I waited a minute for Gray to run around the other side of the house, which was pretty small. When he didn't reappear, I went to look for him.

He was in the backyard, lying facedown in the grass and groaning.

"Gray! Are you okay?" I yelled.

"No."

"Are you frozen?"

"No, Pix," said Gray, rolling over. "But I tripped over my own shoelace. Did you do that?"

Had I felt the whisper of a breeze in my head? "I'm not sure," I answered. "I asked for you to stiffen and fall. I'm sorry."

"Well, I fell," said Gray, grinning. "So maybe it worked a little." He got up and brushed himself off. "Do you want to try again? I don't mind falling for a good cause." He laughed at his own joke.

"Can't. I've got to go inside and get cleaned up before my dad gets back." I started for the house, and stopped. "Thanks—I think."

"Anytime," Gray replied.

CHAPTER THIRTY-FIVE
Ye olde Quack-up

"I'm dying of boredom," I told Mom as we unloaded the dishwasher together on Saturday morning. Except for the "experiments" with Gray, I hadn't been out all week. Most of the time, I hadn't minded reading, watching TV, and writing in my notebook. But suddenly I couldn't stand it a moment longer.

Destiny seemed as bored as me. She tore up the newspaper in her pen and beat her wings till the pieces fluttered all over the mudroom. She wouldn't stop pulling at the cuffs of my pajamas. She needed a change, too.

"Well, you've only got one more day in prison," said Mom, putting an arm around me. "I guess you're looking forward to going back to school on Monday?" She made it sound like a question.

"Sort of." I put my head on her shoulder. "I'm a little nervous. I bet everyone will think I'm an idiot for not catching the softball."

"I doubt it. No one on a bus expects a ball to come flying at them."

Hearing Mom say it like that made me giggle. "It *was* weird," I said.

She thought for a moment. "Why don't you ask Alexa and Lucy to come over tomorrow? I bet you'll feel better after spending some time with them."

The next morning Lucy, Alexa, and I sat together in one of the window seats in our living room, munching the warm strawberry muffins Mom had baked.

"That bruise makes you look kind of cool," said Alexa, studying me as if I were a painting.

My hand automatically went up to my face. "Oh yeah. I bet now everyone will want one."

"I wouldn't mind—if I didn't have to get hit first,"

said Lucy. "It makes you look brave."

"But I'm not really," I objected. "I'm worried about what everyone will say tomorrow."

Lucy and Alexa looked at each other.

"What?" I said.

"You tell her what happened," Lucy said.

"Okay." Alexa held up a finger till she finished chewing. "At lunch on Friday Sage came over to our table. At first she pretended to be worried about you. But then she started saying that you were always trying to call attention to yourself. She said that was why you didn't duck when the ball was coming—and why you have a weird pet instead of a dog or cat like everyone else."

I looked at Destiny, who was nipping at Mom's potted asparagus fern. Instantly, tears sprang to my eyes.

"We told Sage we knew what really happened and that she'd better shut up or we'd tell," said Lucy. "But you should've heard Leo! He said meanness makes people ugly and that she'd better not look in the mirror or she'd scare herself."

Knowing Leo had defended me made me feel a little better. It also made me blush.

Alexa ran a hand over the purple velvet drapes

surrounding our window seat. "You know, this room reminds me of the dance studio where Lucy and I take hip-hop—especially these drapes and the wooden floor. We could show you some steps if you want."

"Dance! Dance!" Sammy chirped. He'd been on the floor "cooking" with one of Mom's pots and a spoon. Inside the pot was a bunch of little plastic people he called "the meatballs."

"I'm not supposed to do stuff like jumping or spinning yet," I said. "But I could be the DJ."

"No, that's okay," Alexa said. "Let's think of something we can all do."

"How about playing hide-and-seek?" Lucy suggested.

"Me pay! Me pay!" Sammy exclaimed. He was at a stage where he said everything twice.

"Oh, Sammy," I sighed.

"He can be my partner," said Lucy.

"He'll only want to hide," I warned her. "And if you let him hide with you, he'll talk and give you away."

"I don't mind." Lucy grabbed Sammy's hand. "Come on, Sammy. We'll go first."

Alexa and I stayed on the window seat and

counted to forty with our eyes closed.

"Ready or not, here we come!" we shouted.

Alexa pointed at the staircase and I nodded. We'd both heard the steps creaking. We tiptoed up with Destiny right behind us. She was getting pretty good at hopping up steps.

Although we could hear Sammy's voice in my bedroom—"Hee, hee, hee! Me hidin'!"—we pretended to look in other rooms. And when we finally got to mine, he scrambled out from under the bed before we could crouch down to look. "You find me!" he squealed, throwing his arms around my knees.

It was my turn next. While Alexa, Lucy, and Sammy counted, I raced to the bathroom and climbed into the claw-foot tub. As I pulled the shower curtain closed, the curtain rod squeaked.

I could hear Sammy pulling Lucy to my room again, as if it were the only place to hide. But Destiny led Alexa straight to the bathroom. Des had honks of surprise, honks of joy, and honks of complaint. This time, her long honks—*Honnnk! Honnnk!*—made her sound as if she were calling me.

"So you think she's in here, Detective Destiny?" asked Alexa, yanking the curtain open.

When she saw me, Destiny went quackers,

honking and flapping. I climbed out of the tub and got down on the floor with Des. She flew onto my shoulder and then onto my head.

"You could use her for a shower cap!" Alexa exclaimed.

"You can't do that with a golden retriever," said Lucy from the doorway.

"Woof!" said Sammy.

We all cracked up, even though the joke was pretty lame.

And for the rest of the afternoon, we kept repeating that line over and over—*You can't do that with a golden retriever!*

It made us laugh every time.

CHAPTER THIRTY-SIX
Ye olde Family connections

"I want to sit with Sage," I told Gray on Monday while we waited for the bus.

His face closed up tight as a fist. "Sage! Why?"

"I have to find out something." There wasn't time to explain more. The bus was already pulling up.

As I climbed the steps, a wave of panic almost made me turn back. The driver was a substitute. If the kids started up again, Mac wouldn't be there to help me. But I had to stick to my plan. So I walked quickly until I got to Sage.

She was too busy examining her hair for split ends to notice me coming. Her mouth dropped open when I sat down.

"Surprise!" I sent her a sly, sideways glance I'd practiced in the mirror.

"Wh-what do you want?" Though she was trying to sound like her snotty self, her voice shook a little.

"You broke our deal. You broke my face, too. I want to know why!" Actually, the swelling under my eye was mostly gone. All that was left was a touch of pink and yellow. If I'd been a sunset, I would have been pretty.

"I didn't throw that ball! Raffi—"

"I know you told him I could stop it with my mind," I interrupted. "You knew he'd do anything you asked him to."

"Well, my grandma's in the hospital because of your mother and her stupid play."

I couldn't believe what a jerk she was being! "Look, I'm sorry your grandma's in the hospital because *she's* a really nice person. But it didn't happen because of my mom. Maybe it made you feel better to see me get hurt, but I'm sure it didn't help your grand-mother one bit. I bet if she knew what you did, she'd feel worse."

"You're not going to tell her, are you?" She looked around the bus to see if anyone had heard me. But the only ones watching us were her friends, Maya, Anna, and Ellie. If I wanted to, I could get them all in trouble. I sent them a look that let them know I was thinking about it.

"That depends." I lowered my voice. "I don't want you talking about me to anyone again . . . or . . . or . . . I'll use my power on you. Got it?"

"Yes." She nodded quickly and went back to examining her hair. I pulled *Ella Enchanted* out of my backpack and pretended to read. But I was thinking that I didn't want to use my power on Sage or anyone else. Ever.

When the bus lurched to a stop in front of our school, I nearly slid off the seat.

"You!" the driver barked as I was about to get off. "Wait here! The office wants you to fill out an accident report."

"Um, okay," I murmured, although the last thing I wanted to do was go over what had happened again.

"We'll stay with you," Alexa offered when she and Lucy got up front.

"Oh no, you don't. She'll have an excuse for coming late to class. *You* won't. Move along, you two!"

My friends sent me sympathetic looks as they shuffled down the steps.

"Tell Ms. Tomassini I'll be in soon," I yelled after them.

"You okay, Pix?" Gray asked, stopping next to me.

"She's fine," snapped the driver. "Don't hold up the line."

Leo was right behind Gray. Before he jumped down the steps, he rolled his eyes at the driver. I put my hand over my mouth to hide my smile.

While the rest of the kids were filing out, the driver found a form and a pencil stub and handed them to me over her shoulder. I skimmed the form quickly. There was a section that asked for information from my doctor and a signature from my parent or guardian. "Excuse me? I think I'm supposed to bring this home," I said.

The driver watched the last kid, a first grader, get off the bus. Then she took off her hat and sunglasses. "You're probably right, kiddo," she said turning around in her seat.

"Aunt Doris!" I jumped up and hugged her. I guess part of me wanted to make sure she was real.

She hugged me back so tightly, I think she was relieved to see me, too. "I'm sorry I was away so long, but I had to do a lot of digging to find out what I needed to know. Our lineage ladies are very good, but they're old and slow. And the documents we have are so faded they're hard to read. It took a while to figure out the puzzle of you."

"What did you find out?

"That your great-great-great-grandmother was a stopper, too, kiddo. It can be a very useful gift, once you learn to control it."

Useful? Huh! Maybe if I was a spy or a ninja. Why couldn't I have gotten a more practical power, like the ability to keep people like Sage from hurting my feelings?

As if she'd read my mind, Aunt Doris said, "A gift like yours takes time to grow into. A Goose Girl's special power appears between the ages of ten and fourteen. That's when our girls become apprentices. They're actually the ones who are responsible for creating the magic that goes into our cakes. We Goose Ladies teach them how to put it all together."

"I don't see how being a stopper can help me bake a cake—unless it's used to stop it from burning in the oven," I grumbled. "Besides, I need to be ready now! I think Raveneece came to my house yesterday. I found Destiny's cowgirl hat on the mat."

"Well, why didn't you say so!" Aunt Doris pursed her lips like Mom did when she was thinking. When she finally spoke, there was anger in her voice. "She's trying to draw you out. She wants you to find her. But you mustn't do it! Even if she manages to get Destiny somehow, you've got to stay away from her, Pixie."

I wrapped my arms around myself to keep from shaking. "Why does Raveneece want Destiny anyway? My dad says she won't lay eggs for another whole year."

"She isn't just after goose eggs. She wants *you*." Aunt Doris sighed. "Look kiddo, Raveneece is out to settle a very old score. She thinks you can help her get back something her ancestors lost long ago."

A lump of fear rose in my throat. "Her ancestors were the Sinister Sisters, weren't they?"

"Yes." Aunt Doris shook her head disapprovingly.

"My mom has this book—*Sister Goose's Cautionary Verse for Brats*. Do you think they wrote it?"

Aunt Doris took a big gulp of air—and swallowed her gum. She coughed so much, her face turned red.

"I thought they'd all been de-destroyed!" she sputtered as I pounded her on the back. "That book is the last and only thing Mother Goose's sisters wrote before they lost the family legacy. Raveneece seems to think you can help her get it back."

"The book? She can have it!"

"The book won't satisfy her, kiddo. It's much more complicated." Aunt Doris looked out the bus window. "In another month when school is over, and if we can convince your parents, you can spend the summer at Chuckling Goose Farm. I promise I'll tell you what I know then. In the meantime, stay away from Raveneece Greed. Now you'd better go to class."

CHAPTER THIRTY-SEVEN
Ye olde Return

Lucy, Alexa, Gray, and Leo were waiting by the class-room door when I got there. But once I walked into the room, a lot of other kids rushed over. Everyone was talking at once, welcoming me back, asking how I felt, and saying they'd missed me. Even two of Sage's friends, Ellie and Anna, were part of the group. Ellie handed me a cute bracelet she'd woven and Anna gave me a pack of gum. It was weird how having an accident could turn you into a popular kid. It made me hope the bruise on my eye wouldn't heal up too fast.

Though I could feel Raffi looking at me, I refused to look back. But on his way to the paper-recycling bin, he dropped an envelope on my desk. Inside was a card with a dog chewing a sneaker. The printed message said, "Sorry! It didn't even taste good." Underneath, Raf had scribbled, "Sorry!" about twenty more times and signed his name.

"Okay, everyone. I agree it's great to have Pixie back, but please return to your seats now," said Ms. Tomassini. She sent me a special smile. "I have good news for you, Pixie. The deadline for the poet laureate submissions was last Friday, but we got it extended for you."

Great. I pressed a hand to my forehead and tried to look as if I were in pain. "I'm sorry, Ms. Tomassini—I forgot about it."

"No worries. You can work on your poem now, while the rest of the class starts their book reports."

I really did try to think of a new idea, but I'd already used up my energy on the bus, dealing with Sage and what Aunt Doris had told me. Anyway, I still wanted to write about Destiny—this time without saying a word about golden retrievers.

"My Destiny"
by Pixie Piper

You can't walk my pet on a leash.
Go fetch, you can't get her to play.
She can't lay an egg, or sit up and beg
But I'm not giving her away.

Suddenly my head started hurting. I'd only rested it on my desk for a moment, when Ms. Tomassini appeared beside me. Like a lot of teachers, she could sneak up on you, quiet as a cat.

"What's wrong, Pixie?"

"I hate my poem," I whispered.

She put a hand on my shoulder. "Would you like me to show you how to write a haiku? We worked on those while you were out."

"No thanks." Before I could stop it, a tear leaked out of my eye.

"Maybe I shouldn't have asked you to try writing yet. Even sitting and listening can be hard when you're recovering from a head injury. Do you need to go home?"

"No," I whispered, even though I really, really wanted to.

I was kind of relieved there was a different substitute bus driver on the way home. I was too tired to think about the Goose Ladies. All I wanted to do was curl up in bed, cuddle with Des, and close my eyes.

The bus seemed to take forever to get to our stop. I said good-bye to Gray and dragged myself down the driveway as if I were crossing the desert. Before I reached for the doorknob, it opened by itself. Sammy squeezed out and grabbed on to my leg.

"Peeksie! Peeksie! Dessie go bye-bye!"

"Whoa, easy, Sammy! You'll knock me over." Then I realized what he'd said.

Mom was staring at me. Her face was too pale and her eyes were too bright. It was a warm day, but I went cold with fear.

"What's wrong?" I whispered.

"Destiny is missing."

"No! No!" I screamed. "She can't be!"

Tears were running down Mom's face. She put her arms around me. "When we came home a few minutes ago, I looked in the mudroom. Des was gone and the side door was ajar. I guess one of us could have left it unlocked, but I don't see how she could have gotten it open. She'd have to be able to turn the knob and push."

Suddenly, I wasn't tired anymore. "I've got to look for her right away! I'm going to the pond."

"No, Pix. You're still healing. You need to rest for

a while. Daddy is already out looking for her. Give him a chance."

"Please, Mom! What if a hawk or a fox finds her? I promise I'll rest later."

"Go to your room and lie down now." I'd never heard my mother sound so strict. I knew it was because she was scared.

I threw my backpack down and stomped up the stairs with my brother behind me, wailing. "No, Sammy—stay out!" I yelled, closing the door on him. It was mean, but I couldn't help it. I flopped on my bed, taking deep gulps of air to stop from crying. *I'll just rest for five minutes and then I'll call Gray,* I told myself.

But five minutes later, it felt as if my mattress had turned to quicksand. I could barely lift an arm or a leg. My head seemed enormous, my neck as weak as a stem. And when I closed my eyes, pictures of Destiny drifted by like a train made of clouds.

Des tugging my pants . . . splashing and chuckling in the bathtub . . . flapping ecstatically when she found me during hide-and-seek . . . sitting cozily on my lap, her heart pulsing against my hand like a tiny star. All the things I hadn't put in my poem, the things that mattered—and now she was gone.

* * *

Sammy was already in bed when Dad finally came home. "I searched until it was too dark to see much, even with a flashlight. But I didn't find anything. Not even a webbed footprint." He looked so sad with the corners of his eyes and mouth turned down. "I'm sorry, sweetheart."

"Thanks for looking, Daddy." I got up from the table and my untouched mac and cheese. "May I be excused?"

Mom gazed at me for a long moment. "Pixie, she might be okay. She might have found shelter somewhere safe for the night."

"Or she could have met some wild goose friends," Dad added. "Geese are social creatures."

I shook my head and forced a smile. "I know. I'm just really tired."

I took the phone into my room and called Gray. He was quiet while I told him what happened.

"I just don't see how Destiny got out," he said finally.

It was hard for me to say what I was thinking. I didn't want it to be true. "It—it must have been Raveneece. She wanted Des really badly." I didn't tell him what Aunt Doris had told me—*that she wanted me, too.*

"Destiny's super smart. She might have gotten away."

"If she did, she would've come back, Gray. Or my dad would have found her when he searched the woods."

"We should look again tomorrow after school. Maybe he missed a clue or something."

"No, we need to look tonight—we can't wait!" I whispered. "We'll go after everyone's asleep."

CHAPTER THIRTY-EIGHT
Ye olde Night Predator

A few minutes after midnight, I heard Gray's *Who-WHO, Who-WHO* call, which sounded something like, "Who-cooks-for-you?" He'd learned the call from a pair of barred owls that lived in our woods, and he was really good at it.

With my parents' permission, I'd been sleeping downstairs on the sofa. I'd told them it was so I could hear Destiny honking, in case she returned in the middle of the night. They'd agreed so easily, I'd felt guilty. But I already had my clothes on under my pajamas. All I had to do was pull off the PJs and slip on my hoodie and sneakers. I'd already tucked the wish cookie I'd saved from the fun fair and the little goose-shaped flashlight into the hoodie's pockets, in case I needed them.

The small wedge of moon over the yard looked like the thin slice of lemon Mom liked to put in a glass of water. As soon as I stepped outside, Gray emerged from the shadows.

"Hi! What's in the backpack?" I whispered. It was bigger and bulkier than the one he took to school every day.

"Wilderness stuff," he answered. "First-aid kit, hatchet, air horn, and wolf urine spray."

"Why would we need wolf urine spray?"

"My dad got it last year for the camping trip he took with his old college roommates. He said they used it to keep moose out of their campsite. But it says on the can that it also repels large predators like bears and coyotes."

"There aren't any bears or coyotes around here, Gray."

"Yeah, but if we see Raveneece, we could spray it at her. When I sniffed it I almost hurled. You want to try?"

"Um, no thanks. I believe you."

Gray burped. "Okay. Let me know if you change your mind."

We jogged across the backyard to the edge of the woods. The dark was different there—something we had to push our way through, like strong wind or deep water. I turned on my goose flashlight. The thin beam seemed almost useless.

"It's still our woods," I said, trying to make myself feel braver.

"Yeah," replied Gray. He slipped off the backpack and fished around inside it. "But I'm getting out the wolf urine just in case."

I pulled the wish cookie from my pocket and broke it in two. "Here," I said, handing him half. "Before you eat this, make a wish . . . but don't say it out loud."

He shoved it in his mouth without asking any questions. "This is stale," he complained.

He was right. I wished for courage before I swallowed my half, but my insides were still doing the hula. It made me wonder if wishes could go stale, too.

We followed the path to the pond as best we could. Weirdly, the trees I knew in daylight looked like strangers now. Some were bent and spindly, with branches that reached out like arms. Others were tall and thick as giants, waiting to munch up trespassing humans like us.

Gray kept squatting to search under bushes as we made our way down the trail. But he only scared up a few mice.

"Destiny!" I called over and over. "Where are you?"

Then, as we neared the pond, Gray grabbed my arm. "Look!" He pointed at two gleaming bits of gold in the tall grass.

Fox eyes! *Braver than brave*, I told myself. I put my hands on my hips to make myself seem larger, and stomped closer.

"Where is my gosling?" I demanded. "Show me before I freeze you solid again. This time you won't be waking up so quickly."

"Pixie, that's a *fox* you're talking to," Gray whispered.

The fox watched me for a moment. It swished its tail back and forth, as if it might be making a decision.

"Come on, Sweet Tooth, take me to her," I said.

But the fox suddenly twitched its ears, turned, and leaped into the pond.

"Wait! Come back!" I called. I could hear little lapping sounds as it paddled through the still, black water. It wasn't long before it disappeared into the darkness.

We rushed into the grass where the fox had been hiding and began to search. It was so swampy one of my sneakers came off my foot and got stuck in the mud. By the time I retrieved it, both shoes were muddy and one of my socks was soaked.

"She's not here," I whispered.

"Well, she *was* here," Gray replied. "Look!" He held up the little cowgirl hat.

I took it and pressed it against my cheek.

"Come on, Pix, don't think the worst," said Gray. "At least we found a clue. That's something."

He was right. But it wasn't enough.

CHAPTER THIRTY-NINE
Ye olde Second clue

I hoped Aunt Doris would be driving the school bus again the next morning. But Mac was back, with a smile and a sniffle. I guess he'd been sick after all.

As I walked up the bus aisle, I passed out copies of a flyer Dad and I made.

Dad had been out early, tacking flyers onto the utility poles along our road. He also said he'd put them up on the bulletin boards in the supermarket and the hardware store in town.

I sat down next to Leo and handed him one. In

the photo, Des was wearing her cowgirl hat and looking straight into the camera. But the flyer was black-and-white. You couldn't tell that her beak and feet were bright orange, her eyes crystal blue, and her beloved hat was red. I wondered if Leo would ever get a chance to see her as she really was.

MISSING!!
Small white goose
Answers to the name Destiny
Please call if you see her.
The Piper Family
Acorn Cottage
555 - 5555

"Do you want me to help you search for her later?" he asked.

"Okay, sure. Lucy, Alexa, and Gray are coming over, too." Actually a lot of the kids on the bus had volunteered to help look.

Ms. Mosely posted the flyer on all the electronic bulletin boards around school. During the morning announcements, she even got on the speaker to ask everyone to keep an eye out for Destiny.

In the halls and at recess, kids from the tiniest to the oldest stopped to say they'd search their neighborhoods. It was awesome that so many people wanted to help. By the end of the day, I dared to believe that she was still out there.

* * *

"Look!" Lucy exclaimed. We'd been searching the woods for an hour without finding anything. But she was pointing through the trees at something white at the edge of the pond. It hadn't been there before.

My heart began flapping like a bird taking off. But the creature's shape wasn't right. Its body was too slender and its neck was a long, curved letter S.

"That's an egret, Lucy."

"Oh, sorry."

"It's okay." I patted her shoulder. "You know, I'm pretty sure Dessie's not here. With all of us calling, she'd have found us by now. Even if she were caught up in a vine or something, she'd be honking for help."

Alexa looked around. "Is there anyplace else we can search?"

"We never checked out the toilet museum," said Gray.

"My dad went there the first day." I realized that didn't sound very hopeful, so I tried again. "I guess she could have found her way there by now. Let's go."

If you started from the top of Winged Bowl's driveway, you could follow it down past Acorn Cottage to the bottom of the hill. From there, it divided in two.

The left drive in the fork led to Uncle B.'s big house and the right to the parking lot for the Museum of Rare, Historical, and Unique Toilets. But you could also get to the museum by taking the path through the woods and walking around the pond, which was what we did.

The pebbled walkway that led to the museum's entrance was lined with tulips, daffodils, irises, and other spring flowers. Every few feet there were benches for visitors to rest on. It was pretty right up to the decorative toilets on either side of the door—not antiques, just ordinary ones. Each toilet sat on a stone pedestal and was planted with bright red geraniums. At Christmas there were mini trees with twinkling lights in those toilets.

We circled around the outside of the building, looking behind the shrubs and in the clumps of flowers, but we didn't find a single white feather. When we got back to the front, we sat on benches across from each other—boys on one, girls on the other. The museum was only open on weekends, except for summer and the winter holiday season, when it was open every day. I could have asked Uncle B.'s permission for us to go inside, but really I just wanted to go home. Even though they didn't say so, my friends seemed to understand.

For a few minutes we sat there quietly. Then Gray said, "Remember when we came here on the third-grade trip?"

Since Winged Bowl Elementary and Middle School had been built, every third-grade class had visited the museum to learn about "sanitation, health, and human ingenuity."

"Of course I remember!" said Alexa. "Someone pooped in the rare, historical, and unique toilets."

"It was Play-Doh, Al," said Lucy.

Gray whooped. "I thought Mrs. Hill was going to faint when she saw it!"

"Did you do it?" Alexa asked, raising an eyebrow at him.

"No! It must have been someone in Ms. Martinez's class."

"I had her," Lucy said. "But I don't think anyone in our class did it."

"Actually, it was me."

We all looked at Leo as if he'd just spoken Gnomic or Ogrese.

"You're kidding!" Gray said.

"Nope." Leo shook his head. "I had this new Play-Doh set and I was fooling around mixing colors. So

I tried red and blue and got purple. And I mixed red and yellow and got orange. Then I tried red and green—"

"And you got brown," said Lucy.

"Right," said Leo, nodding. "And since we were going to the museum the next day, I decided to make some art to put in it."

"Art?" Alexa said.

"Well, yeah. It seemed like a good idea back then. I made three, um, snakes, and put them in a plastic baggie in my jacket pocket."

Gray giggled so hard he slid onto the ground, writhing like a worm in a hot frying pan. Leo looked down at him and grinned before he continued. "Once our class was in the museum, I told Ms. Martinez I needed to use the restroom. On my way there, I placed my snakes in my three favorites—the dragon toilet, the turtle toilet, and the train toilet."

I could feel my face getting red. "Why?" I asked.

Leo shrugged. "I wanted my work to be in a real museum."

"But you hurt Uncle B.'s feelings," I said. "He feels the same way about collecting toilets as you do about drawing." I don't know why I said that. Uncle B. hadn't been there. When everyone was laughing, it was me who'd gotten hurt feelings.

Leo gave a sorry little shrug. "It was third grade. I probably wouldn't do it now."

"I know, I know," I said, sniffing. "I'm not mad at you."

Lucy patted my hair. "You can't help it. You're upset about Destiny," she whispered. It was something my mom might have said.

Alexa handed me a tissue. "Lu and I need to go back to your house. My dad is going to pick us up soon. If you want, we can search again tomorrow."

I took a long breath to clear my head. "Okay. I need to get home, too." Without another word, we all got up to leave.

Be brave, have hope, I told myself as I led the way around the pond and up the path through the woods. Then I fell.

"Pixie!" Lucy squealed.

"It's okay—I didn't hit my head this time," I said, trying to sound cheerful. I got up and scanned the ground. "There!" I said, pointing. "I tripped on that root."

"Did you hurt your ankle?" asked Gray. "Leo and I could carry you. I know how to make a really cool four-handed wilderness seat."

"Thanks, but there's nothing wrong with my ankle."

"Are you sure?" He sounded a little disappointed.

"I'm fine." I looked around at my friends. "Please don't mention this to my mom. She'd kill me if she found out I fell."

We laughed a little about moms and worrying as we started walking along the path again. But when no one was paying attention, I took a long look over my shoulder. Was it the same root Sage had tripped on? I wasn't sure. But I felt like maybe I'd discovered a clue—an important one.

CHAPTER FORTY
Ye olde teapot

After Sammy was in bed, Mom set a pot of tea and her acorn mug on the table. I was still there, lingering over the mint chip ice cream I was having for dessert. "What are you thinking about?" she asked, pulling out the chair opposite me.

"Roots, actually," I said, planting my spoon in the ice cream.

Mom cocked her head and gave me a look that was half questioning, half comical. "Explain, please."

"Well, a tree root popped up on the path in the woods. I was just wondering why."

"I know roots sometimes surface when they're searching for water or oxygen," said my mom. "But I suppose it could also be that it's suffering from too many people trampling over it. That root has probably been working itself up for a while—sort of like a blister on a toe. Only now it's become a big-enough bump to notice."

"It's not exactly a bump." I lifted the lid on the teapot. "It looks more like this handle—a loop of twisted root."

Mom took the lid from me and examined it. "Huh. This handle does look like a root."

I nodded. I was so used to seeing the ivy green teapot that I'd never really looked at it. Now I studied the leafy design that had been etched all over it.

"So this belonged to your great-grandma?" I asked.

"Maybe to my great-great-great grandmother. I don't know how far back it goes. But I hope someday it will be in your kitchen."

I didn't want to think about that. "Both family roots and tree roots can be pretty powerful," I said, changing the subject. "I mean, they affect the lives of so many future people and future trees."

Mom took a sip from her mug. "They are really

important. I wish I knew more about mine. Ours, I mean."

I felt a flush creep up my neck. It seemed unfair that I knew so much more about our family history than my mother did. I couldn't help thinking how good it would feel to tell her everything. But I was afraid if I did, it might bring her harm. I couldn't bear it if anything happened to her because of me.

I slurped the melted ice cream from the bottom of my dish. "I guess I'll go finish my homework," I said.

"Okay, my little sapling." Mom took a last sip from her mug and stood up. "Maybe I should tell your dad about that root before anyone trips over it. Tomorrow he can remove it."

A mountain range of goose bumps popped up on my arms as I thought of going back into the woods that night. But I had to find the root before Dad cut it out. What if it really was a clue—the one that would lead me to Destiny? I knew it could also be a trap. And that whoever set it might be waiting for its prey like a spider in a web.

I was the prey.

For some reason I imagined a dark space beneath the ground where Destiny was alone and terrified. I knew if I asked Gray, he would come along, but Des was my gosling and Raveneece was my problem. I had to be braver than brave. I had to go alone.

This time I was glad the night was so dark. If Mom awoke, I didn't want her to see me cutting down the clothesline—and using her best sewing scissors to do it. But if I was right about the root, I was going to need a long rope.

It was surprisingly easy to find it again. If anything, it seemed to have pushed farther up through the soil, which was really creepy. But I had to know if it would lead me to Destiny. So with shaking hands, I kneeled down, wound the rope around it, and tied a tight knot. Then I stood back and yanked it as hard as I could. When the ground moved slightly, I pointed my light at the space. I could just make out a jagged circle of dirt about the size of a manhole cover. The root was right smack in the middle, making it look a lot like a giant version of Mom's teapot lid.

I yanked the rope again—and again. Finally I was able to drag the chunk of earth far enough away to uncover the hole. Panting, I threw myself down on the ground and crawled over to peer into the blinding blackness. I couldn't tell how deep it went. Ten feet? A mile?

"Destiny!" I called quietly. "Des!"

Nothing. Not a honk or a squeak. A tear dripped off my chin and dropped into the nothingness. But the truth was, part of me felt relieved that I didn't have to climb down into the hole—that I could still go home to my family, our cozy cottage, and my bed with the patchwork quilt.

Then I heard something slow, soft, and mournful. *Honnnnk. Honnnnk.* Destiny! I aimed my flashlight into the hole.

It was a long way down. So long, my weak light could hardly reach bottom. But I could make out some kind of cage. And inside it, a small white head.

CHAPTER FORTY-ONE
Ye olde Wretched Reunion

My heart curled up like an inchworm just thinking about descending into that hole. But Destiny was down there and I had to get her. I waved my light around and spotted a ladder made of branches tied together with dried vines. I couldn't quite reach it, but if I hung on to the rope and shimmied down backward, I thought my feet might touch the top rung.

They did.

I climbed down for what felt like a very long time, holding my breath the whole way. When I finally got to the bottom, I was in a small, round room with a dark, narrow hallway leading off it. From somewhere back there, I heard a sound like the clattering of pots and pans. I had to hurry!

The room itself was bare, except for a table, two chairs, and the cage that held Destiny. Her head was lying on her breast, as if she had no idea I was there. Quickly, I squatted down and poked a finger through the bars.

"Dessie, it's me." I rubbed her head, but she didn't move. The lock on the cage had a key in it. I unlocked it quickly, shoved the key in my pocket, and lifted her out. She was as limp as a feather pillow. "Des, wake up," I pleaded.

The clattering sound got louder and I smelled smoke. I had to go right away. With Des cradled in my arms, I whirled toward the ladder— *and screamed*! Raveneece was standing in front of it. At her feet was her fox.

"I've been expecting you, brat," she said, showing her pointy, picket fence teeth. She was wearing a stained white cook's apron over her black jumpsuit. She still had the nest on her head.

"'Beware of the hat where a birdie did bed,'" I remembered Mom reading.

Well, it was too late for that now.

"I don't get many visitors, but I'm always prepared just in case," said Raveneece in a voice sweet enough to give you a cavity. She held up a tray with a teapot, a plate of burned cookies, and a candle.

"I—I'm not visiting," I said. "I came for my goose." I tucked Des under one arm and took a step backward.

Raveneece set her tray down on the table. "What's your hurry? Don't you like it here? I decorated it myself."

I gazed at the bare dirt walls. "Do you l-live here?"

"My sisters and I dig traps—I mean, homes—wherever we need to be. It's a talent of ours."

"So all your, um, homes are underground?"

"Certainly. There's so much more room to expand down here. Who needs the sky when you can look up at a lovely dirt roof?" She began to recite in a creaky voice:

"The cleverest sister lived in a cave
And not in a dirty old shoe.
She hated the sight of the stars and the moon
So only a dirt roof would suffice!"

Raveneece tapped her foot, as if she were waiting for a compliment. "Well, what do you think?" she asked finally.

I swallowed. "It's a very nice poem. But didn't you mean to say, 'only a dirt roof would *do?*'"

"Why?"

"Because *do* makes the poem rhyme." Slowly I began to recite:

"The cleverest sister lived in a cave

And not in a dirty old shoe.

She hated the sight of the stars and the moon

So only a dirt roof would *do!*"

Raveneece scowled at me. "Who told you I wanted it to rhyme?"

"No one. Sorry." I glanced at the ladder. If I pushed her out of the way, I might be able to climb fast enough to get out before she caught me.

As if she could read my mind, Raveneece grabbed a rickety rung. "You like my handiwork? You'll have plenty of time to examine it later. Now put that goose back in the cage and let's have a snack."

"Can't I hold her? She seems sick. Has she had any food or water?"

"Hmm . . . let me think." Raveneece put a finger to her lips. "NO, NO, AND NO!" She snatched Destiny and shoved her back into the cage, leering over her shoulder. "If it will make you feel better, I can give her some company." She snapped her fingers. "Sweet Tooth—get over here!"

The fox slunk up beside the table. Its bright yellow eyes were fixed on Destiny.

"No, please!" I cried. "Don't!"

"Then have a seat."

I pulled out a chair.

"That's right. Mind your Auntie Raveneece and everything will be fine."

"You're not my aunt!"

"Of course I am. We're part of the same family."

I shook my head. "Aunt Doris told me you're descended from the Sinister Sisters."

"Every family has its differences, brat. But we're related whether you like it or not. Just think—you and I could be the ones who make peace. Wouldn't that be nice?" Raveneece reached out to pat my head. When I jerked away, her lips curled in an awful snarl. "Aunt Doris is a liar. My sisters and I aren't sinister—we're the ones who've been wronged. Cheated by our own relatives, the Goose Ladies. When you hear the entire story, you'll understand."

I tried to smile. "Okay, maybe some other time, *Aunt* Raveneece. But now, I'd better go home or my parents will be worried."

"You can go home *after* you've helped me. Now,

eat! We have a lot of work to do."

I looked at the gray, ashy cookies. "What's in them?"

"Just the usual." She reached under her nest hat to scratch her head.

"Eggs from the birdies, honey from the bees
Spiders' legs and crickets' knees
Mix with flour, stir in soil.
Leave 'em in the oven till, um, till
    the worms all bake."

Not *bake—broil*, I thought. Leave them in the oven till the worms all broil.

But this time I didn't tell her.

"No thanks," I said. "I might be allergic to them. I've never eaten dirt or bugs."

"That's because your family can buy plenty of flour, brat. White, wheat, whatever! But my family doesn't have that luxury. And do you know why?"

I shook my head no.

"Because our own flesh-and-blood sisters, the Goose Ladies, refuse to share their good fortune. Only *they* can bake wishing cakes. Only *they* decide who gets them. If they'd let my sisters and I sell a few, we could afford nice things, too. But those miserable misers have never given us a single cake."

I looked down at my lap. "Goose Ladies don't sell wishing cakes. They give them away randomly. They do it to help keep hope alive."

"*Pfoo!* They're just a bunch of foolish do-gooders. My sisters and I are businesswomen. We're planning to go into the cake-selling business as soon as we recover our birthright. And *you* are going to help us!"

CHAPTER FORTY-TWO
Ye olde Missing ingredient

Raveneece's underground "home" was as dark as a bat cave. It had no windows. The hole I'd come down the ladder through was too small and too high up to see the moon or the stars. I had no idea how long I'd been down here or if a single ray of light would reach us once the sun rose.

I felt like putting my head down on Raveneece's table and bawling. I didn't know how to bake a wishing cake, even if I wanted to. "You've made a mistake," I told her. "I don't know anything about baking."

She stared down her nose at me. "I'm not interested in your culinary skills, brat. It's rhyming I'm after. Why else would I keep you?"

"But anyone can rhyme," I whispered.

Raveneece's eyes got so narrow, they practically disappeared into her face. "Unless someone steals their gift!" she growled.

It took me a moment to understand. "Do you mean Mother Goose? Why would she do that?"

"I told you she was selfish! She didn't even think of what would happen to her poor sisters after she disappeared from town. She just left those girls with no means of supporting themselves. But did they give up and starve?" Raveneece looked at me as if she expected an answer.

"I—I guess not," I said, hoping it was what she wanted to hear.

"Of course not! Greenteeth, Nettlehair, Ninetoes, and Fishbreath were resourceful girls! They decided to write their own book of rhymes—and not another volume of vomitous verse for infants, either." She sat up proudly. "The book they produced was more practical—*Sister Goose's Cautionary Verse for Brats.*"

"We have a copy of that book at home," I said, careful to keep my voice steady.

"Then you know what good rhymes the sisters wrote. Much better than Mother Goose's goo-goo, ga-ga, choo-choo stuff! Tell me your favorite."

"I didn't finish reading them," I admitted. "They scared me."

Raveneece smirked. "That's because they were supposed to! Greenteeth, Nettlehair, Ninetoes, and Fishbreath wanted to write a book that would teach children everywhere the consequences of not obeying their elders. One reading and the little brats would become cheerful servants, working day and night to avoid the punishments described in those rhymes." She pointed a crooked finger at me. "But do you think the world appreciated what a wonderful gift it had been given?"

"No?"

"No!" Raveneece slammed the table with a fist. Two cookies bounced off the plate and landed on the floor near the fox. Sweet Tooth sniffed them and backed away with her tail between her legs.

"The few books they did sell got passed around town. Everyone who read them—the ones who could read—began having nightmares." Raveneece broke into a grin that showed all her greenish teeth, and she rubbed her hands together. "The sorriest folks were the foolish, weak-hearted parents who'd read the book to their children. As word spread, the sisters never sold another copy." Raveneece sent me a sly look. "Now, what would you do if you were them?"

"Um, maybe I'd forget about poetry and try to earn money babysitting or something."

Raveneece sighed and shook her head. "Wrong! They decided to bake wishing cakes! They'd spent years watching their older sister do it, and now it was their turn. Oh, they knew it would be more work than book writing, but they wouldn't be foolish like their do-gooder sister. They were out to earn money and fame." Raveneece leaned across the rickety table, so her face was closer to mine. Her breath smelled like dead mouse. I edged my chair back and pretended I was stretching.

"Greenteeth, Nettlehair, Ninetoes, and Fishbreath called their bakeshop Mother Goose & Sisters," continued Raveneece. "They knew the name alone would have people lining up to buy their wishing cakes. Of course, it was the least the old lady owed them."

"But selling wishing cakes would have spoiled her mission to spread hope," I said. "It wouldn't have been fair."

"Fair, shmair! Was it fair that when the old goody-goody learned of their plans, she used one of her own wishing cakes to destroy the rhyming ability of her sisters and their descendants forever after?"

"Oh-h-h! So that's why you can't rhyme," I said. Quickly I put my hand over my mouth.

Raveneece took a cookie off the plate and examined it. "You think it's funny?"

"No. But I—"

Suddenly Raveneece flung the cookie across the table. It hit me in the cheek like a slap.

I put my hand to my face, but I didn't let myself cry. Sweet Tooth had been curled up under the ladder, but at the sound of that slap she lifted her head and watched me. I sat stony-faced as Raveneece poured our tea.

"Let's toast, brat," she said, lifting her cup. "Starting tonight, what Mother Goose stole from us will be returned by you—*her direct descendant*. You're going to teach me to rhyme. Oh, it really is such delicious revenge!"

I swallowed the burning lump in my throat. "If I do, will you let me and Dessie go home?"

"Oh, I'll let you go home, all right. Once I've

learned the secret to rhyming, I won't need you or your goose." She glanced at Dessie. "Though I doubt that bird will be fit for more than roast goose pie. She doesn't look as if she'll live through the night."

CHAPTER FORTY-THREE
Ye olde Lesson

"Sweet Tooth! Watch the brat!" yelled Raveneece as she disappeared down the tunnel for pencils and paper. But it wasn't really necessary—I wasn't going anywhere without my gosling.

Would it be possible to teach Raveneece to rhyme? Weren't all the descendants of the Sinister Sisters under a wishing cake spell? Raveneece seemed to believe I had the power to break the spell—maybe because I was a direct descendant of Mother Goose. To save Destiny and myself, I would have to try.

In a moment Raveneece was back with a few crumpled sheets of paper and some pencil stubs. "Here. Now let's get started." She threw the supplies on the table.

I took a deep breath. "Okay. I think we should start with word families. This one is called AT."

"Never heard of them," grumbled Raveneece. "Are they part of the secret of rhyming?"

"Oh, yes," I said, as I wrote a list:

AT

cat

bat

pat

mat

rat

hat

sat

"These words sound alike," I explained. "You can use them to make a simple rhyme. Try this one:

"The cat sat on the . . . ?"

"Couch," said Raveneece.

"No, you have to pick a word from the list. Try again."

"Cat." Raveneece crossed her arms over her chest. *"The cat sat on the cat?"*

"Sometimes they do!" she snapped.

I sucked in my bottom lip. "Um, let's do a different one. This is the IG family." I turned the paper over and wrote:

IG

pig

big

dig

fig

wig

"Okay," I said. "The pig is . . . ?"

Raveneece tapped her nails against the table while she thought. She looked up at the ceiling, where I could see a bat roosting in a rocky crevice. "Pink!" she said finally. She searched my face with her sunken eyes.

"Um, close," I said, hoping she wouldn't get mad. "But to make a rhyme, you should pick a word from the list."

She pouted like a toddler. A really ugly one.

"Come on, take another look." I pushed the list under her nose. "The pig is . . . "

"Wig?"

"The pig is wig," I repeated. "Well, it does rhyme."

Raveneece adjusted her nest hat. "See? I'm a fast

learner." She tapped her pencil on the table. "Come on. What's next?"

I thought for a moment. "Since you're doing so well, let's move on to a three-letter rhyming family— the AKEs. This group includes one of your favorite subjects."

She watched closely as I wrote the next list.

AKE

snake

bake

lake

cake

wake

"Okay, here we go," I said. "I want to bake a wishing . . . ?"

Raveneece frowned as she looked at the list. "This one is hard."

"Try each word out before you choose. Take your time."

"I want to bake a wishing *well*?"

"Um, good try, but it doesn't rhyme. You need to pick a word from the list, remember?" I tapped the paper.

"What was the question again?"

Tears crept into the corners of my eyes. It was

starting to seem like I might never get out of this dark, ugly place. I thought about what Ms. Tomassini might do. "Let's look at the list together," I suggested. I put my finger down next to the word *cake*, hoping she would take the hint. "I want . . . to bake . . . a wishing . . . ?"

"S-s-snake!" said Raveneece. "I want to bake a wishing snake."

"Uh, well, that's . . . pretty good." I pushed back my chair and stood up. "I think you're catching on. I'd like to go home now. I'm really tired."

Raveneece clucked her tongue. "I'll be the one to decide when we're done, you lazy brat. Now sit down and let's keep going."

I sat down and faked a big yawn.

"All right, brat—you can go to sleep. *Here*."

"But I have to go home or my parents will go crazy with worry. I'll come back here tomorrow after school. I'll bring you some flour, too."

"You'll go home. Someday. But first you're going to help me bake some wishing cakes. It should go faster now that I can rhyme, too. After we've made a hundred or so, I might consider letting you visit your family."

CHAPTER FORTY-FOUR
Ye olde cracked Aunt

Raveneece carried the candle and the tea tray to the entrance of the long, dark tunnel. "Follow me. I've filled a ditch with sticks and leaves just for you. You might get some termites in your hair, but you can comb them out in the morning."

I gripped the edge of the table. "I won't be able to sleep without Destiny. And if I don't sleep, my brain will be too muzzy to do any more rhyming. Please let me take her along."

Raveneece hesitated. "Oh, all right," she finally

said. "You can have your goose." She set the tray down and stomped over to the cage. I held my breath, wondering if she'd notice that the key was gone, but she didn't seem to remember it.

"No goosey snack for you yet, Sweet Tooth," Raveneece said, shooing the fox away. "The brat needs her bird to sleep." With one hard yank, she pulled Des out.

"Please be gentle," I pleaded.

Raveneece lifted Destiny and shook her. "What's the matter, goosey? Wake up!"

Slowly Destiny raised her head and looked around. She seemed dazed, and I wondered if she would ever be the same perky little goose again. Then, without warning, she lunged forward and bit down hard on Raveneece's nose.

"Oh! Ooh! Ouch! Owwwwch!! GET HER OFFFF!!!" Raveneece shrieked. She was struggling to pull Destiny away, but Des had her beak clamped tight as the vise in Dad's workshop.

I kept my arms at my sides, fists clenched. "Promise to let us go and I'll make her stop!"

Instead, Raveneece dug her fingers deeper into Destiny's feathers. Des fought back harder, too, beating her wings madly as she struggled to get free.

Then, as Raveneece staggered back, I saw Sweet Tooth slink around behind her and stretch out on the ground. With her next step back, Raveneece tripped over her. Shrieking, she went down on her backside—and Destiny slipped out of her grasp.

Sweet Tooth was on our side!

I scooped Des up and began climbing the wobbly ladder. Halfway up, I glanced over my shoulder. Raveneece must have had the breath knocked out of her, because she was sitting on the dirt floor. I was almost to the top when the ladder began to sway wildly. I looked down and saw Raveneece standing there. "Come back here or I'll shake you off, brat. It's a long fall down."

"Fly, Des!" I screamed, tossing her up toward the sky. I wasn't even sure she could fly that far, but she flapped her wings and made it through the opening.

For a moment my heart lifted. Then I looked back down. Raveneece was holding a broom. The handle was made from a branch, and instead of straw at its end there were a bunch of long, white feathers.

Raveneece smirked and swung the broom at the ladder. She struck it so hard my entire body vibrated. One more hit and I was sure the rickety contraption would splinter.

"You'll pay for letting that goose loose!" she shrieked.

I was about to fall and break into a zillion pieces, but all I could think about was that she'd finally made a rhyme. Too bad she didn't know it.

"Climb back down here or I'll make sure you come crashing down! And when you do, you'll never escape. I'll have you making cakes for me until every drop of your power is gone."

I stepped down a rung.

"That's a smart brat. Come back and I'll teach you how wishing cakes can bring you wealth and power. Just imagine—that little brother of yours can have whatever he wants—his own candy store or a pony. Your family will thank you for it."

"He'd love a pony," I said, stepping down again. In my head, I was gathering the courage to trust myself. I was going to have to be braver than braver than brave.

"Hurry brat, before I lose patience!"

"I'm just resting, Aunt Raveneece. It's a long way down and I'm very tired. But if you want, I'll tell you a rhyme while I get my strength back."

"Make it about a birthday wish!" she ordered.

"Okay. Please give me a second to think up a good

one." I closed my eyes as I hung on to the swaying ladder. I remembered Gray and I experimenting with my stopping power. The tomato juice had streamed into my hair, Hermie the wormie had wriggled down my back, and I wasn't sure whether my stopping rhyme had had any effect on Gray.

"Don't be scared, be angry!" I whispered.

"What's that brat? I can't hear you."

"I'm just thinking out loud, Aunt Raveneece."

I thought about how Mom and Dad would feel if I didn't come home.

I thought about Sammy, who wouldn't understand.

I thought about Gray, who might always wonder if he could have helped me get away.

Then I thought of how Raveneece and her sisters wanted to steal hope—something everyone in the world needed.

The anger inside me smoldered. It was as if my heart had caught fire. In my mind's eye, I saw words swirling like a tornado, rising higher and higher till they spread across the sky for me to read.

"Here's your rhyme," I called, looking down into Raveneece's eyes. Then I chanted each word, loud and clear:

"Halt the hands of clocks and watches

Make the spinning compass cease
Stop the evil in this place
BY FREEZING RAVENEECE!"

Raveneece's mouth was open in surprise. One hand gripped the awful broom and the other was wrapped around the ladder. She was stiff. Immobilized. She was as motionless as a mannequin in a store window.

I had no idea how long she'd stay that way and I didn't want to find out. I reached up and grabbed the clothesline that was dangling from the hole. I tried pulling myself up, but the rope kept slipping through my sweaty hands. I clutched it between my knees, too, but they were trembling so hard, I kept losing my hold. I scrabbled against the wall with my feet, but the dirt crumbled as I tried to dig in and I couldn't get any traction.

I kept on struggling, the sound of my own crying echoing in my ears. And then I heard something else. Honking. I was almost there.

Destiny flapped with joy when she saw me crawl out onto the ground. For a moment I just stretched and looked up at the stars. "Come on, let's go home," I said, reaching into my pocket for my goose flashlight. That's when I felt the key to the cage. I slipped it out of my pocket and held it. I didn't want a single reminder of that awful place, so I flipped it back into the hole.

Ping!

With Destiny safe in my arms, I peeked over the edge and blinked. The key was drifting down the hole in a slow, dreamlike way. It was heading straight for Raveneece. Finally it struck her nest hat and bounced off. I was about to turn away when I heard the sound of something cracking. I covered my eyes, but I couldn't help peering through my fingers. It was Raveneece. She was shattering into pieces.

I screamed and, with Des in my arms, ran toward Acorn Cottage. But the woods had turned into a frightening version of the place I knew. The path seemed to be closing in on me. Spiky, shrubby branches reached out, poking and pricking at my arms and legs. Rocks and pebbles made me slide and stumble. Once I fell to my knees, but even then I held onto Destiny. I could see Acorn Cottage just ahead. There was a light in my bedroom window.

Then I heard a high, heartbreaking cry. Sweet Tooth! I'd forgotten about her. She was still down in the hole. Trapped.

I stopped running. I was panting and shaking, and I wanted to go home so badly it hurt. But I turned and headed back.

The woods were silent as I crouched at the edge of the hole and shone my light into the pit. I saw Sweet Tooth sniffing and pawing around the splintered pieces of Raveneece. She looked up at me and whimpered.

"I've got to go down there one more time, Dessie," I said, setting her on the ground. "She's just a wild creature who got caught by Raveneece. She helped us get away. I've got to save her."

Des plucked at my sleeve with her bill, as if she didn't want me to go. "I'm coming back. I promise," I whispered as I grabbed the clothesline and lowered my legs into the hole. I felt strange—kind of like I was watching myself from a far-off place. The girl that was me-but-not-me began climbing down the ladder again. But once I reached the dirt floor, my senses jolted awake. All around me were pieces of Raveneece—little shards of ear, hair, elbow, knee, finger, toe—as if a life-size statue had been smashed. I was terrified of stepping on any of it.

The little fox was pressed against the wall, her

ears flattened and her tail between her legs. She was just as afraid as me.

"Come on, Sweet Tooth, it's time for you to go home to your real family," I said, stretching out my arms and bending down to pick her up. But as I did, I saw two shiny fragments near Sweet Tooth's paw. They were Raveneece's angry eyes and they were glaring at me. For a moment I felt so weak I could barely stand.

A gentle nudge at my leg made me turn. I looked into Sweet Tooth's golden, trusting eyes and felt my strength returning. When I lifted the fox up, I could feel her trembling. "It's okay, you're safe with me," I whispered.

The ladder seemed even more fragile this time, as if any minute one of the twiglike rungs might break. About halfway up—*crack!*—one of them did. I let out a scream that echoed over and over, but I hung on, one leg dangling in space.

Snap-snap-snap-snap! The rungs were breaking behind me. I was practically stepping on air when I reached the final one. Desperately, I crawled out of the hole with Sweet Tooth under my arm.

Des was waiting for us, murmuring a stream of low, quick honks. For a moment everything was still. Then I heard something like a broom sweeping. Whatever it was stirred a wind that made the trees and grasses sway. It grew so strong it caused the dirt beneath my feet to slide. It was as if someone—or something— was trying to sweep me back into Raveneece's hole!

I lay flat on the ground, kicking and clawing, trying to catch a root or a shrub. I shoved Destiny and Sweetie beneath my body to keep them from being swept backward, too, but the wind gathered force. It roared in my ears and tore at my clothes like a wild beast. I felt it trying to enter my mind and sweep up my rhyming ability.

"NO, YOU CAN'T HAVE IT!" I screamed. And for a moment, my voice was a wind, too—full of thunder and fury:

> "Broom crack! Spell break!
> You'll never get a wishing cake.
> Braver than brave, truer than true
> Sinister Sisters, begone with you!"

Behind me, something began rumbling. I flipped around just in time to see the dirt lid with its root handle come sliding straight toward me. I grabbed Sweetie and Destiny and rolled out of its path. The lid narrowly missed us as it skidded by and stopped right over the hole.

* * *

When I finally stood up, my legs were shaky. But the woods seemed safe and calm again. I leaned down to give Sweet Tooth a last hug. "Go on, Sweet Tooth, go find your family," I said.

She lowered her front legs, as if she were bowing, before she pranced off into the woods.

The pale light of early morning began coloring the world just as Des and I turned and headed for home. Birds were making wake-up calls and wild-flowers were unfurling their petals to catch the dew. The scent of pine needles and moldering leaves, and the sharp smell of new growth, were like perfume to my nose. At the side of the path, two not-quite-ripe wild strawberries hung off their stems. If the rabbits didn't get them first, Gray and I would be back to pick them.

CHAPTER FORTY-FIVE
Ye olde Familily Truths

Acorn Cottage was silent as I carried Destiny upstairs. Although my arms were beginning to ache, I didn't ever want to let go of her again. When I pushed open the door to my room, I saw the outline of someone in my bed. I gasped and squeezed Destiny even tighter.

HONK!

"Pixie!" Mom jumped up and pulled me into her arms. "I was so worried! On my way to start coffee, I peeked in your room—and you were gone! Dad's out looking for you." She kissed the top of my head. Then she kissed Destiny's. "What happened? Where did you find her?"

"She needs food and water right away, Mom," I said. I almost started crying again.

"Oh! Let's get her to the kitchen right now." Mom put an arm around me, and I leaned against her as we walked downstairs.

We fed Destiny and kept on petting her even while she ate. And I still held her afterward, while I sat in Mom's lap. "I want to tell you not just what happened last night, but all of it," I said. "But first we have to talk to Daddy. He needs to know the truth about both of us."

I was done keeping secrets from my parents. The Goose Ladies would have to understand. The next time I saw Aunt Doris, I was going to insist that she talk to Mom and Dad.

"All right, Pixie," Mom murmured into my ear. "Let's call him on his cell. We'll tell him as soon as he gets back here."

Dad thundered through the house and hugged me tightly. Then he took Destiny into his arms, cooing soft words. He always looked like a gentle giant when he held her. I began by explaining about Aunt Doris and the Goose Ladies, with Mom chiming in whenever she could. Poor Dad! He kept holding the top of his head with his hands, as if it might pop off. "I feel as if I'm stuck in a dream," he murmured a few times.

Before I chickened out, I hurried on to tell how and where I'd found Destiny. It hurt to see my parents, with their wild eyes and dazed looks. "You went into the woods at night? Alone?" Dad's voice was hoarse, and he looked as if he might cry.

"It was the wrong decision—a terrible decision— but for the right reasons," Mom said, stroking his arm.

Then I told them what had happened to Raveneece. Remembering the awful scene was almost as hard as going down the hole. When I was finished, I felt horrified all over again. I'd frozen Raveneece so I could get back to the people I loved. But I'd expected her to come back to life and go back to wherever she came from.

"Mama! Dadeee! Peeksie!" Sammy called from his room. I'd never loved hearing his little voice more.

"I'll get him," said Mom, standing up.

Dad sprung up, too. "I'm calling the police," he

said. "Then I'm going to check the woods."

"No! No police, Dad!"

"Pixie, be reasonable . . ."

"But you don't understand! The Goose Ladies are a secret!" I grabbed my backpack.

"Where do you think you're going?" asked Dad.

"I have to get ready for school."

"Oh no, you don't. You're not going anywhere."

"Please, Daddy." I grabbed his hand. "I have to talk to Gray. And I have to tell everyone that Destiny is back."

"You can call them later, when they get home."

"No! I—I need to have a regular day. I want to feel happy again." I began to cry really hard.

Dad held me until I calmed down. "I'll walk you up the driveway," he said, brushing the hair from my eyes. "Then I'll check the woods and call the police."

Dad and I made it to the bus stop before Gray—but someone had gotten there ahead of us. Taped to the pole that held the school bus crossing sign was an envelope with my name on it. I ripped it open and pulled out the note inside:

Dear Pixie,

Please call me—

111-222-3333
Your faithful aunt,
Doris

All this time, I'd never thought to ask for her phone number!

"Look, Dad," I said, handing him the note. "I'll call Aunt Doris after school. You and Mom can both talk to her."

He raised an eyebrow. "Well, it's a start," he said.

"And Daddy? Maybe you could wait to call the police until you talk to her."

"We'll see."

At the sound of a door slamming, Dad and I both looked across the road. Gray scrambled down the steps and ran to meet us. "Hi, Pix! Hi, Mr. Piper!"

"Gray, I got Destiny back!" I yelled.

"Really? Ye-e-ea-a-a-ay!" We both started jumping up and down. I was planning to tell him everything later, but for now it felt good to celebrate.

Squeak, rumble, squeak, rumble. The school bus turned onto our road. Dad stayed at the stop and watched me get on. I took a window seat and waved to him. He stayed there while Mac drove off. And he was still there when we got to the next corner and turned onto the main road.

CHAPTER FORTY-SIX
Ye olde Visitor

At dinner Dad told me he'd spent all day searching the woods. "I checked the entire path, but all I found was this, Pixie." He held up his wrist. A piece of Mom's clothesline was wound around it like a thick rope bracelet. "There's no sign of a root or a hole. Or any *pieces*. I just don't understand it."

"It wasn't my imagination, Dad! When Aunt Doris gets here, she'll tell you." Actually, I could hardly believe Aunt Doris was coming. I'd called her first thing when I got home, and I think even she had been shocked by my news. Because when I'd asked her to talk to my parents, she'd agreed right away. She was supposed to arrive tonight after dinner.

Mom looked at the clock. "I should probably change my clothes before she gets here." She was wearing a tie-dyed T-shirt, love beads, and a scarf tied around her forehead like a headband. Today had been Sixties Day at the senior home.

I thought of Aunt Doris's bus driver cap, her silvery wig, and her fake hairy wart. "Don't bother," I said. "She'll probably be wearing a costume, too."

I was right. When Aunt Doris arrived, she had on her Mother Goose outfit—the one she'd worn at the Renaissance Faire. She and Mom looked at each other and grinned.

"I knew your great-grandmother," Aunt Doris told Mom. "She loved costumes, too."

"Mom's great-grandmother? You mean like my great-great-grandmother?" I blurted out.

"That's right, kiddo."

"But how could you have known her? Wouldn't you have to be really old?"

Aunt Doris cracked her gum. "We Goose Ladies don't look our age."

Mom served tea and oatmeal raisin cookies and joined Dad on the couch. I plopped down on the rug, and Aunt Doris sat in a plump armchair. When she set her black cone-shaped hat beside her on the floor, Sammy ran over to check it out. He never sat anywhere unless it was time to eat.

"Would you like to wear it?" Aunt Doris asked. She helped him put it on and he spent the rest of the evening bumping into the walls and furniture.

"I won't beat around the bush," said Aunt Doris after she'd sipped her tea. "Pixie is very powerful. There hasn't been a case of shattering for more than a hundred years. And since our apprentices' abilities emerge between the ages of ten and fourteen, she could become an even greater force for hope over the next few years."

Mom touched my shoulder lightly, as if I were a priceless painting. "Are you saying the apprentices don't all have the same degree of power?"

"The girls' powers vary greatly. That's why some cakes can grant small wishes and others big dreams." Aunt Doris cocked her head toward Mom. "Did you know the Goose Ladies' power usually skips a generation?"

"No!" Mom looked startled. "But my mama used to say they would come for me!"

"It was her hope, but it was very unlikely. Your mother loved her years as an apprentice. But when she got older, she chose to leave us as many of our girls do. She wanted love and a family."

"So I wouldn't be a Goose Lady forever?" I asked.

"You might choose a different life. Or you might choose to stay," Aunt Doris replied. "But no matter what you do, part of you will always be a Goose Lady."

Dad leaned forward. "I don't know about this. It seems dangerous."

"I won't deny it," Aunt Doris agreed. "But in addition to creating wishing rhymes, the apprentices all have special talents. Pixie's is the power to stop bad things from happening, like the kind of turmoil humans can cause. It's a very handy ability. The Sinister Sisters, on the other hand, have only one talent—causing trouble." She smiled at Dad. "I'd say we have the advantage."

"Raveneece got her down into that hole," he argued.

I couldn't keep still any longer. "It was my own fault, Daddy! Aunt Doris told me to stay away from Raveneece, but I didn't listen. I couldn't leave Destiny down there!"

"Your father is right about the danger, kiddo," said Aunt Doris. "We're certain the Sinister Sisters will want revenge for what happened to Raveneece. That's why we think you should stay with us at Chuckling Goose Farm as soon as school is out. You'd be under our protection. No one will be able to find you there. Of course your parents would have to agree." She looked at Mom and Dad.

I swallowed and swallowed, but the word *revenge* was stuck like a lump in my throat. "Would I be able to take Destiny?" I asked finally.

"Of course! Every Goose Girl brings her goose along. Destiny will love it there. And so will you. Think of it as summer camp with baking. Doesn't that sound like fun?"

Destiny honked as if she approved. We all laughed, which made her honk some more. For a goose, she sure was a ham.

Suddenly I remembered something. "You said the Sinister Sisters just have one talent. But what about the broom?"

Aunt Doris narrowed her eyebrows at me. "You never mentioned a broom, kiddo."

"I think it caused that big wind that almost swept me back into the hole."

"What did it look like?"

I closed my eyes and saw it again. "The handle was a twisted branch and the brush part was made of white feathers." I didn't say "goose feathers" in case Destiny understood.

"The broom of doom," said Aunt Doris in a hushed voice. "I've heard of it, but I didn't know it still existed. I'll have to talk to the other Goose Ladies about it. They might know more."

Mom twisted her love beads around her fingers. "Do you think I should go?" I asked her.

She reached over and took my hand. "I always expected you to join. I just wish it wasn't so sudden." She turned to Aunt Doris. "What about after the summer? Even if Pixie is safe at the farm, what will happen when she comes home?"

"Hopefully we'll have made peace with them by then. Raveneece was a fool, but deep down her sisters know it's wrong to interfere with our apprentices, who are, after all, only children." Aunt Doris stood up. "If we're agreed, I'll get started making the arrangements right away."

Both of my parents nodded, but they looked as if their hearts were heavy.

"Heah." Without coaxing, Sammy took off the

black hat and returned it to his new friend. He was beginning to grow up. Suddenly it felt like everything was happening too fast.

"Wait! Please!" I jumped up. "My friend Gray—I told him everything. I was so scared I couldn't help it."

The look Aunt Doris sent me—skin crinkling around her soft, hazel eyes—was understanding. "It might be best for him to stay at the farm for the summer, too. The Sinister Sisters may be on the lookout for any kid who knows too much."

"Even boys?" I asked.

"Boys have their roles, too, kiddo. I'll speak with the others about him." Aunt Doris grinned as she tied on her hat. Then she put an arm around me. "Now come and walk me to the door."

Mom and Dad took Sammy off to bed. They seemed to understand that Aunt Doris wanted a moment alone with me.

"You're going to be a big challenge, Pixie Piper, but you may turn out to be a great Goose Lady." Aunt Doris looked me in the eye. "Did you learn anything from that horrendous experience?"

I thought maybe I had. "Yes—about my power," I said. "It seems as if the tornado of words that brings a stopping poem only comes when it's super important."

Aunt Doris nodded. "A Goose Lady's gift must be used sparingly and wisely. Now it's time for me to go." She reached for the doorknob.

"Wait—aren't you going to do that disappearing thing?"

She put a finger to her lips and stepped outside. I stood there watching as she faded around the edges, became a soft and fuzzy image of herself, and turned into a sprinkle of glitter.

Maybe someday I'd learn to do that, too.

CHAPTER FORTY-SEVEN
Ye olde Poet Laureate

When Ms. Mosely announced her name, Sage strutted to the front of the auditorium. Her lips were pressed together in a smug smile that made a little part of me wish I'd entered the poet laureate contest just to keep her from winning.

Up on the stage, Ms. Mosely and Uncle Bottoms were beaming like twin spotlights. Then Ms. Mosely shook Sage's hand, and Uncle Bottoms presented her with the medal. As he hung it around her neck, a photographer from the local paper snapped a photo.

Tomorrow she'd be smiling at me from the front page of the *Winged Bowl News*.

Big whoop.

Our teachers led us in a round of applause. Some of the kids were stamping their feet and shouting, just because they could.

"Quiet!" hollered Ms. Mosely when it started to go on too long. "I'm sure you're all anxious to hear Sage read her prize-winning poem." She signaled Sage to begin.

Sage stepped in front of the microphone and lowered it like a pro. "My Little Angel"—by me," she began.

"Clippity clop her nails wake me up
Then she barks until I rise.
Like a windshield wiper she wags her tail
And doggy-kisses my eyes.

"Sometimes she chews our chair legs
Which makes my mother sore
But though Angel gets sad, she never gets mad
'Cause she'd rather play than roar.

"On days when the house is empty
And there's no one to talk to or care

I never moan, though I eat alone

Because my Angel is there."

Of course, we had to clap again. But I had to admit Sage's poem wasn't bad—which was super annoying.

She was walking off the stage when Ms. Mosely caught her by the shoulder. "Hold on! There's still one more honor for you. Mr. Bottoms will tell you about it himself."

Uncle Bottoms stepped forward. "That's right! I'm going to give you your first official assignment as poet laureate."

Sage's eyes seemed to grow bigger. I thought I saw her gulp.

"The Museum of Rare, Historical, and Unique Toilets has a very exciting announcement," Uncle Bottoms told the audience. "One of the most famous commodes in the world, the throne toilet that belonged to King Louis the fourteenth of France, is now a part of our collection."

Uncle Bottoms stepped back from the mic so we could applaud the toilet. I didn't mind clapping again because I suddenly had an idea what Sage's assignment was going to be. It made me pretty cheery.

"The museum will be holding a special ceremony on the last day of school to unveil this priceless piece of history," Uncle Bottoms continued. "As the first poet laureate of Winged Bowl, Sage, you will write an original poem in honor of the throne toilet. And you'll be my special guest at the event where you'll read your work before the public."

Whoopie!

CHAPTER FORTY-EIGHT
Ye olde Secret Deal

After Aunt Doris met with my parents, there were new rules. I had to come straight home after school every day for the next two weeks, which was when school ended. It meant that I wasn't allowed to go to any parties, not even Alexa's. The excuse I told anyone who asked was that I was being punished for sneaking out in the middle of the night to find Destiny. At least it was a little bit true.

I didn't argue. I'd been seeing the broken pieces of Raveneece in my dreams each night, especially her eyes. And I still heard the sweeping sound—or thought I did—whenever I felt a breeze. I wondered if it was the broom of doom. And if it had swept up those pieces of Raveneece.

To help me keep busy, Dad had given me a special trunk to pack my things in for Chuckling Goose Farm. But I still missed my friends. Now that it was almost summer, they got to do things like go biking or swimming after school. Mom knew I was lonely, so she tried hard to be home more.

"Anything new today?" she asked when I walked in the door on the day of the big announcement.

I plopped my book bag on the kitchen floor and went to get a glass of water. "Sage Green won the poet laureate contest."

Mom made a little *hmm* of surprise. "You never know who's got poetry inside them."

"Oh, Mo-om!" I rolled my eyes. "Destiny and I are going up to pack now."

Sammy grabbed my leg. "Me pock!"

"Sure," I said, taking his hand. The truth was, he liked to unpack what I'd just put in my trunk. But it didn't matter—I had all afternoon. Besides, I was doing a lot of unpacking of my own. Twice I'd tucked in my poetry notebook and pulled it out again.

Okay, so I was pretty sure all the other apprentices at Chuckling Goose Farm would write poems, too. But some of mine were about feelings that were private. Others were just plain silly. I wasn't sure any of them were good enough to make me an apprentice.

For the third time, I stashed the notebook underneath my PJs. Then I rolled up Leo's drawing and put that in, too. I also added my lucky goose flashlight and the new copy of *Ella Enchanted* Mom had bought for me. Since I'd gotten into the habit of reading it each night to help me sleep, my copy had gotten pretty tattered. I was leaving it home so it didn't fall completely apart.

Sammy toddled off to his room and brought back his teddy bear, his nursery rhyme book, and a few diapers. When he plopped them in the trunk, I realized he thought he was coming with me. I had to squeeze my eyes shut to keep them from tearing up. But maybe someday he'd go to Chuckling Goose, too. As Aunt Doris had said, "Boys have their roles."

Mr. Westerly wasn't too keen on Gray going to Chuckling Goose with me. My parents and I had a meeting with Gray, his dad, and his grandma.

We didn't tell them everything. But we did explain that Chuckling Goose offered lots of fun and interesting activities like caring for farm animals, gardening, baking, magic, horseback riding, fishing, and performing community service. And if you got picked to go, it was free.

"Why did they choose Gray?" asked Grandma Westerly.

"The owners are relatives of Dana's," my dad replied. "I told them what a wonderful kid he is and how helpful he's been to me here at Winged Bowl."

Gray's grandma smiled at Mom. "Oh, Dana, I didn't realize you were related to them. That's different!"

Huh. I hadn't thought about the Goose Ladies being Mom's relatives, but it was true.

"I'd rather keep an eye on my son myself," said Mr. Westerly. He looked at Gray. "I can take you fishing."

"But Dad, you're at work all week," Gray pointed out. "Besides, I really want to go!"

"Rob—it's a farm," Grandma Westerly said calmly. "Gray will have fun and be safe. It will be good for him."

Gray's dad finally agreed to let him go. Reluctantly.

The plan was for Aunt Doris to pick us up at the toilet museum on the night the King Louis was being unveiled. She said since our friends and neighbors would be busy, it would be easier for us to slip away unnoticed.

Still, every time the phone rang, I got nervous. I was afraid Mr. Westerly would make Gray cancel. So when Mom appeared in the doorway, saying, "Phone call for you," I nearly dropped the trunk lid on my fingers.

"Is it Gray?" I asked.

Mom shook her head. "Nope, it's Sage."

"Tell her I'm not here," I said, without even bothering to whisper. Mom left the phone on my desk anyway. Then she led Sammy away, promising him a cookie.

I eyed the phone. I knew if I didn't answer, Sage would probably just call back. So I grabbed it and squeezed it like it was her neck. "It's me. What do you want?"

"Pixie, I made a mistake."

You made a lot of mistakes, I thought. But I was silent, so she'd have to do the talking.

"I don't want to be poet laureate. I never should have entered. I want you to have the medal."

"But I never even entered," I said.

"That's because you got hit in the head."

"Yeah, thanks to you."

"I'm sorry, Pixie—really I am! You could still write a poem and give it to Ms. Mosely tomorrow. I'll go with you to help explain."

"Look, there's nothing to explain. I don't want to be poet laureate, either. The difference is, I don't have to. Enjoy your golden donut." I hung up.

The phone rang again.

"Oh, please, Pixie! Please! You've got to help me. I can't write a poem about a toilet. But you live next door to the museum. You're used to them. You know what to say."

I thought about reminding her that she was used to toilets, too, especially since there were seven bathrooms in her house. You could say she *lived* in a toilet museum. But I didn't feel like being mean anymore. I ran my hand over one of the stitched squares on my quilt. It was a piece of an old apron Mom used to wear—a print of a cow jumping over the moon. After everything that had happened to me, it almost seemed possible.

"I'll help you write it," I said finally. "But I won't read it at the ceremony. You'll have to do that yourself."

"But—" Sage sounded as though she was about to argue. Then she stopped herself. "Thank you, Pixie."

CHAPTER FORTY-NINE
Ye olde Great Unknown

I watched Sage follow Uncle Bottoms up onto the stage of the museum's community room where the star of the evening, the King Louis throne-with-a-secret, was waiting. Sage lifted the skirt of the ruby red gown my mom had made her so she wouldn't trip on the stairs. With the golden donut around her neck and her grandma's tiara in her shining black hair, she looked like a genuine princess.

There was such a big crowd that some people in the back had to stand. My entire class was there, as well as a lot of other kids from our school, and our teachers and parents, too. And almost all the residents of Good Old Days had come, because Mom's theater group was going to perform a few songs from *Grease* as part of the evening's entertainment. Of course, some people were there just to see what a throne toilet looked like.

Uncle Bottoms cleared his throat. "Good evening everyone," he said into the microphone. "Thank you for coming to help celebrate the museum's newest treasure." He waved a hand at the King Louis, which had a big red ribbon wrapped around it like a present. "This is a special night for all of us. From now on our town will be recognized as the home of one of the world's most historically important commodes."

The audience clapped. Gray let out a loud burp of appreciation. Ms. Mosely turned around to glare at him. It was a good thing school had ended today or he might have gotten a detention.

"Before we move onto the evening's other festivities, we have a special treat," Uncle Bottoms continued. "To commemorate the museum's latest and greatest loo, our poet laureate, Sage Green, is going to recite her original poem."

When she didn't move, Uncle Bottoms gave Sage

a gentle nudge. Her eyes darted around like two gup-
pies that had just seen a shark, until her gaze settled
on someone in the front row. Grandma Gloria! I saw
her give Sage a thumbs-up.

Sage walked to the front of the stage, smiling.
When she began speaking, her voice sounded as
grand as if she were King Louis's granddaughter for
real:

"I am a princess as you can see
From crown to gown, I'm pure royalty
But a princess can't sit just anywhere
She needs a throne, no simple chair.

"It must be a thing of perfect beauty
But also a place to do her duty
Proclaiming laws to rule the lands
Knighting knights and giving commands.

"Oh, I am a princess, as you know
A princess who really has to go!
My legs are crossed in deep despair
Until I spy a royal chair.

"A coat of arms upon its back
It's not for any local hack.

Polished to a sunny shine
This chair is truly very fine.

"But best of all beneath its seat
Is something practical and neat.
A bowl that's hidden till I need it
Now please excuse me . . . GET LOST,
    BEAT IT!"

Sage pretended to shoo the audience away with a wave, just the way she'd practiced at my house. For a moment there was silence. Then Uncle Bottoms let out a great guffaw. It spread through the auditorium like a wave, until everyone in the room seemed to be laughing.

Gray sent me a sideways look. "Sage is getting awfully good at writing poetry."

"Shh!" I jerked my chin toward the stage, where Uncle Bottoms was passing a pair of scissors the size of a barbecue fork to Sage. They were so heavy he had to help her use them to cut the red ribbon on the royal potty.

When I heard the soft scuff of a door, I looked back over my shoulder. A figure in a hooded black cape had slipped inside the room. Her face was in shadow, but I could see a lock of frizzy red hair peeking out. It was Aunt Doris.

I leaned closer to Gray and whispered in his ear. "She's here. It's time for us to go."

Gray looked back toward the door. "Is that *her*?"

I nodded.

"Did you find out where it is?'

"Unh-uh. They never tell anyone." I looked back again "She's waiting. Des is already out in her van with our trunks. Ready?"

"Yeah. I guess." Gray was breathing quickly. He'd fought so hard to get permission from his dad, I was surprised he was nervous.

I stood up and reached for his hand. "Braver than brave," I whispered as I gave it a squeeze.

"Truer than true," he replied.

Pixie's Notebook

SAMMY POEM 1

Moses supposes his toeses are roses
Plump little raisins, delicious to eat.
But Sammy supposes that toes go in noses
Better for smelling his own stinky feet.

GIRL IN A BLACK HAT

There was a young poet who lived in an acorn
(You thought I would say a shoe)
With her mom, dad, and bro,
   and an egg sure to grow
There wasn't too much that was new.

Until the egg cracked and out came a goose
With blue eyes and feathers all white.
But instead of honking, the goose came out talking
At first all it said was "Write!!!"

Then as it got older, the goosey got bolder.
It ordered the girl to get busy.
"For verse I've a yen, so with keyboard or pen
You must rhyme until you get dizzy!"

With the goose for a master,
   the girl wrote much faster
Till a mountain of poetry grew.
Then she put on a hat, very pointy and black
And away the goose and girl flew.

THE BROOM OF DOOM

If you're cracked to pieces
And there's no way you can mend
The broom of doom can help you heal
Though it is not a friend.

It may put you back together
But you won't know your own face
For your eyes and ears and other parts
May not fit back in place.

SAMMY POEM 2

His hair's a nest for food
He cries to get his way
He's the center of attention
Whenever friends come play.

So why do I wait while he takes a nap,
For Sammy to wake up and climb in my lap?

HAIKU FOR MS. TOMASSINI
BY PIXIE
(5 syllables – 7 syllables – 5 syllables)

Night. Geese are leaving.
Wings beat against moon, saying
Good-bye, Destiny!

HAIKU BY DESTINY
Honk! Honk! Honk! Honk! Honk!
Honk! Honk! Honk! Honk! Honk! Honk! Honk!
Honk! Honk! Honk! Honk! Honk!

FOR MS. TOMASSINI—
BURPING LIMERICK
Gray Westerly burps like a champ.
He burped so much he got a cramp.
The doctor said, Stop!
Or your stomach will pop
Then on Gray's lips Doc put a clamp

HAPPY HEAD LICE AWARENESS MONTH!

To keep the critters from our hair
Hats and combs we mustn't share.
They're hard to see, those lousy lice
The adults like a grain of rice.
So if your scalp you have been scratching
It might mean teeny lice are hatching.
Then to the nurse you must repair
To let her check your itchy hair.
And if they're calling your head home
You'll need a special kind of comb
And shampoo to destroy those lice.
That's all of my lice advice!

A LETTER

Dear Chuckling Goose,
I think I'll like you
But I wonder if you'll like me?

Mom says I'm impulsive
Gray calls me cranky
But I know there's more I can be.

If the world I could shake
With a cake that I bake
I'd feed everybody a share.

And when all ate their fill
They'd be full of good will
So that for Mother Earth they would care.

Read on for an excerpt
from Pixie's next adventure,

Pixie Piper
and the
Matter of the Batter

Pixie Piper
and the
Matter of the Batter

Annabelle
Fisher

CHAPTER ONE
ye olde escape

Riding shotgun in Aunt Doris's truck, with my goose, Destiny, on my lap, I stared out the window and tried to memorize landmarks. Woods, lakes, schools, firehouses—they were all starting to look alike. In the backseat my best friend, Gray, was sitting with the twins, River and Rain, and their goose, Drizzle. We were on our way to Chuckling Goose Farm, but the only one who knew what town or even what state it was in was Aunt Doris. Unfortunately, she could keep a secret better than a safe can keep a fortune.

Although Aunt Doris called the twins my cousins, I'd never met them before. It made us all a bit shy with each other. But Gray tried his best to be friendly by telling goose jokes.

"Why do geese fly in a vee?"

"I give up," answered River after less than a second.

"'Cause it's too hard to fly in an *s*."

"Hah!" River forced a polite laugh.

"This one's better," Gray promised. "Why do geese fly south for the winter?" He didn't even wait for the twins to answer. "Because it's too far to walk!" He cracked up. I laughed, too, so he wouldn't feel bad.

After a while Aunt Doris said, "You kids should probably try to get some sleep. We've got a long ride ahead." But there was still an hour of daylight left, and I wasn't a bit tired—until she began humming something that sounded like a lullaby. Fortunately, she still popped her gum occasionally. Aunt Doris was a real thunder-mouth, and those cracks helped me to stay awake.

I don't know how long we'd been riding when something strange happened. The truck, which Aunt Doris called Babe, was passing through filmy clouds that looked as if they'd been spun from thread as fine as spider silk. *Clouds?* I looked around and realized we were driving on a skyway rather than a highway. I glanced over at Aunt Doris. She'd put on a pair of thick goggles and was concentrating hard on the road, so I rolled down the window just enough to sneak a pinky out and snag a strand of cloud.

After that we began descending, not like a plane

getting ready to land, but straight down like an elevator. As far as I could see, there was only the sea beneath us. I looked back at Gray and the twins, but they were sleeping. If I woke them, Aunt Doris would notice. For some reason it seemed important not to let her know I was up.

Just before we sank below the waves, Aunt Doris leaned over and closed my window tightly. I held my breath as the truck slipped below the surface. But when I couldn't hold it anymore, I discovered I could breathe anyway. We drove past a coral reef, where two green turtles were foraging. A school of banana-yellow fish swam alongside us for a while. But when a giant red squid tried to grab us in its tentacles, Destiny honked in alarm. Aunt Doris cracked her gum and stamped down hard on the gas pedal.

Whoosh! We shot up through the surface of the sea and rolled onto an island. My heart stopped pounding—until the ground beneath us began to quake and rumble.

Earthquake? Volcano? I wasn't sure. Then the island slapped its enormous tail.

"Hang on!" Aunt Doris whispered. I held Destiny closer as we were launched into the sky by the whale's powerful spout. We whizzed through the air until we finally landed on an icy mountain peak, sharp as the point on an icicle. Babe rocked dangerously back and forth on its tip. That was when Aunt Doris shut off the engine. "I need a nap, kiddo," she said calmly. "I suggest you take one, too."

CHAPTER TWO
Ye olde Unidentified Flying objects

"We're here," announced Aunt Doris, adding a gum crack for emphasis.

I opened my eyes and discovered we were parked in the driveway of a white farmhouse with a big front porch and a red barn beside it. A gaggle of geese honked a greeting. Destiny raised her head and fluttered her wings.

I stroked her soft back and murmured, "It's okay, those geese are going to be your friends."

"Everybody out!" Aunt Doris ordered cheerfully. "I'll find Wyatt and ask him to help with your trunks." She headed off toward the barn.

It felt good to stand up and stretch my legs. I gazed around and saw two long picnic tables. One held platters of food. There were towering stacks of pancakes and waffles taller than me.

Two girls who'd been setting the tables dropped

spoons and forks. "Hello! Welcome!" they shouted, running toward us.

For a moment I just stood there in awe. These girls were apprentices. Real, live *Goose Girls*. They were braver than brave and truer than true.

The older apprentice, a teenager with the long golden hair of a storybook princess, grinned at us. "Hi, I'm Perrin. We're really excited to have you here."

I smiled back. "Thanks, I'm Pixie."

"Oh, I know."

Hmm. I wondered what she she'd heard about me. "Do you also know Gray, Rain, and River?" I nodded toward the others.

"Now we do!" exclaimed the second apprentice. "And my name's Pip." She had sandy hair that was cropped short around her elfish ears. She looked about our age or a bit older.

"You must be starved. It's been a night and a day since you've eaten." Perrin took me by the arm.

"But I had dinner last night—pizza. That's what we always have on Fridays," I told her.

"Last night was Saturday," Perrin said. "This is Sunday morning."

I blinked. Had I really slept for a night and a day?

I caught River and Rain sending each other amazed looks.

"Well, I'm starving!" exclaimed Gray. "And the food looks awesome."

A new Goose Girl ran past the table. She was waving a butterfly net at a flock of fluttering, um, well, I wasn't sure what.

"Whoa! I've never seen butterflies like that before," said Gray.

"They're not butterflies. They're naughty biscuits!" she shouted, swinging the net. "And you're welcome to eat any you can catch."

"Oh, Nell!" Perrin shook her head. "Did you make the biscuits too light again?"

Gray's baby blues bugged out. "You mean those are flying biscuits?"

"Yes, unfortunately." Nell sighed.

"Too bad I don't have my catcher's mitt," Gray said. But he stretched up his arm like he was playing outfield and jumped. "Gotcha!" he crowed. He broke the biscuit in two and offered half to me. The salty, buttery crumbs melted on my tongue.

Rain and River began chasing the biscuits, too.

"Hello, cousins!" another voice called. With my cheeks bulging like a chipmunk's, I turned to see who'd arrived. A very tall girl was waving a net at the flying biscuits. Her thick, waist-length braid whipped across her back.

"Oh, Winnie, I added too much rising powder again," Nell told her.

"Don't worry, I'll catch them. Though it wasn't just the rising powder, you know." Winnie smiled fondly at Nell and began to chant,

"When baking biscuits rich and buttery
A heart that's light will make them fluttery
The joy that fills you helps them rise
And sends them off to sunny skies."

"It's true," Nell told us. "It happens whenever I get overexcited."

I looked around. "What were you overexcited about?"

Nell's dark eyes grew round and shiny. "Why, because you were coming, Pixie. I never met a hero before."

I felt my face grow hot. I knew my freckles were spreading from my cheeks to my ears. "I'm not a hero," I mumbled.

Perrin put a hand on my shoulder. "What you did was very brave. You eliminated our worst enemy."

"But it was an accident," I croaked. "I didn't mean to shatter her."

"Tell us how you did it," Pip pressed.

"Were you afraid?" Nell's voice quivered.

"Girls! Didn't I warn you not to bombard Pixie first thing?" scolded Aunt Doris as she returned from the barn with a long-limbed teenaged boy.

"Sorry Aunt Doris," Pip said. Nell clapped a hand over her mouth.

"Hello, new girls, I'm Wyatt," the boy said to Rain and me. Then he bumped fists with Gray and River. "It's about time we had some more guys around here. I hope you two like geese, 'cause you're going to be my assistants in the barn. We're in charge of egg production."

River and Gray both beamed.

"I thought you kids would have devoured these by now," said Aunt Doris, eyeing the waffle and pancake towers. She yawned loudly. "I'm going up to bed. Perrin, Winnie—please show Rain and Pixie the way to the kitchen when you're done eating. The rest of the Aunts are anxious to meet them."

We tucked into breakfast as though we hadn't eaten for months. Everything was as delicious as it looked. Besides pancakes, waffles, and naughty biscuits, there were bowls full of berries that glistened like jewels. The butter was creamy. The syrup shone like amber light. And no one asked me any more questions about how I'd shattered Raveneece.

While I ate, Destiny sat on my lap. I let her sip from my water glass and fed her berries from my plate. Rain and River's goose, Drizzle, walked around the table nibbling grass. But Destiny squawked when I tried to put her down, too.

"Has your goose always been shy?" asked Perrin.

"Not with my family or friends. But she's never met other geese," I replied. The thing was, Des had become clingy ever since we'd been trapped in Raveneece's hole in the woods. But I didn't want to bring that up. Talking about what had happened still gave me the creeps.

"She'll get used to the others," said Wyatt.

"I know. She just needs some time," I agreed. "I'll keep her with me till she's ready."

Wyatt sent me a sorry look. "The Aunts have a no-geese-in-the-farmhouse policy."

"Oh." A lump rose in my throat. "Des has been sleeping with me every night since we escaped."

"Don't worry, the boy's bunkhouse is right next to the barn. Gray, River, and I will be close enough to hear her if she wakes up at night," Wyatt said.

I nodded. I could tell he'd be kind. Besides, Des loved Gray almost as much as me.

When Rain and I were so full we were holding our bellies, Perrin said, "If you're done, let's go to the kitchen so you can meet the Aunts."

Winnie nodded. "Yes, they're very anxious to meet you. But they wanted us to get acquainted first."

We slid off the bench. Wyatt stood, too, and I settled Destiny in his arms. "You're going to have fun with other geese," I told her.

But when I turned to follow Perrin, I heard Wyatt yelp.

"Yeow!"

We spun around. Wyatt was sucking on two fingers. Destiny was already fluttering at my feet.

"Oh no! Did she bite you? I'm sorry," I told him.

"It's okay," he answered. "But she sure has a strong bill."

"I know. It's what saved us." I picked up my gosling and looked into her crystal blue eyes. "You need to go with the boys now, Dessie. I'll see you later."

"I'll take her," Gray offered.

I nodded and gave her to him. "Have fun, Des," I whispered. "Please."

Don't miss
Pixie Piper and the Matter of the Batter,
by Annabelle Fisher

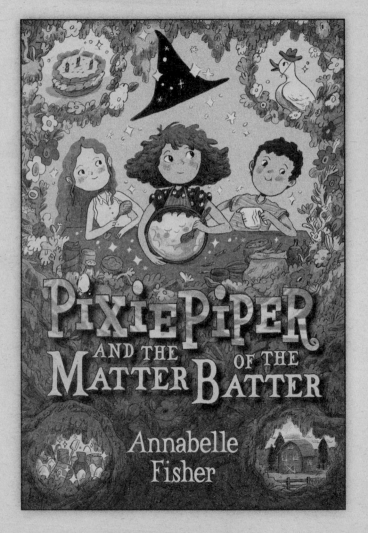

 Greenwillow Books

An Imprint of HarperCollins*Publishers*

www.harpercollinschildrens.com